Never had she felt such precise scrutiny of her face until this moment. The man was prying deep within to seek the truth. Would he find what he was looking for? Was this the same look he had used to read his victims before seducing them into his arms?

Armand swiped a defeated fist through the air. "You don't want this marriage any more than I do. That is correct?"

Madeleine shrugged and looked away, only to have him jerk her chin and her eyes back into his cage of vision. "You do not, Madame, I can see it in your reluctance."

"Please."

He studied her for the longest time. He did not trust her. One falter to her stare, and he would know Madeleine was not being truthful. But something, that tiny flinch in his left eye, wanted to believe her.

And that was all she needed, a moment of doubt, of wanting to believe.

"Very well. Let it not be said Armand Saint-Sylvestre isn't a formidable opponent. I shall remain with you. . . . But . . . !"

Madeleine flinched at the deep declaration. She had expected a *but*. She'd stepped into smoldering ash when agreeing to this, knowing that from that point on any move she made would only flame the embers.

"There was mention of *anything*."

"I do recall saying that, Monsieur." She also recalled that had not been part of the script. Mention of *anything* had been a moment of panic on her part. "What might your definition of the term be?"

Armand walked toward the bed, hands crossed in front of him. He plopped into the thick feather-stuffed mattress and patted the velvet counterpane.

This man's challenge set her blood to a slow and heavy drift within her veins.

<u>BOOK YOUR PLACE ON OUR WEBSITE</u> <u>AND MAKE THE</u> <u>READING CONNECTION!</u>

We've created a customized website just for our very special readers, where you can get the inside scoop on everything that's going on with Zebra, Pinnacle and Kensington books.

When you come online, you'll have the exciting opportunity to:

- View covers of upcoming books
- Read sample chapters
- Learn about our future publishing schedule (listed by publication month *and author*)
- Find out when your favorite authors will be visiting a city near you
- Search for and order backlist books from our online catalog
- Check out author bios and background information
- Send e-mail to your favorite authors
- Meet the Kensington staff online
- Join us in weekly chats with authors, readers and other guests
- Get writing guidelines
- AND MUCH MORE!

Visit our website at
http://www.zebrabooks.com

Lou Betty

BETRAY ME NOT

Michele Hauf

Michelle

Hauf

Zebra Books
Kensington Publishing Corp.
http://www.zebrabooks.com

ZEBRA BOOKS are published by

Kensington Publishing Corp.
850 Third Avenue
New York, NY 10022

Copyright © 2000 by Michele Hauf

Zebra and the Z logo Reg. U.S. Pat. & TM Off.

First Printing: September, 2000
10 9 8 7 6 5 4 3 2 1

Printed in the United States of America

For my dad, Marv Enerson,
and for Donald and JoAnn Hauf
with love

One

Versailles, 1662

It took mere seconds for Armand Saint-Sylvestre to resign himself to the fact that he was being kissed. With great passion.

She had appeared out of nowhere. He had only glimpsed the black-velvet mask, the vivid blue irises within the cut-out circles, and the sparkling masses of crimson-copper curls that showered upon her shoulders.

At first contact, soft feminine lips to his mouth, Armand reached up with both hands, ready to push the woman away, but instead he stumbled clumsily backward until his shoulders connected with the stone garden wall behind him. A few nonsense syllables growled up from the base of his throat, and then with a resolute sigh, he ceased protest. He might be leaning a bit south for the quantity of wine he'd indulged in this evening, but he was no fool.

Closing his eyes, Armand concentrated on the amazing power of the kiss. Her actions demanded satisfaction. The woman—

this mysterious woman—slid her tongue inside his mouth to dance. An exquisite surge of want spread through his body, awakening—and stiffening—his need.

Who was this vixen who had fallen brazenly into his arms? Did it even matter?

Not for the heady sensations that coursed through his body, it did not!

Her kiss tasted ambrosial, a hint of melon, a sprinkle of cinnamon. Persimmons. He'd noticed them earlier on the buffet tables lining the formal gardens of the south parterre here at Versailles. King Louis XIV was too impatient to wait for the builders to finish the landscaping surrounding the cozy hunting lodge. "We must have a fête!" His Royal Highness had declared.

Always another fête.

Courtiers festooned in damask and diamonds, and soldiers on leave, now danced and frolicked beneath the citrus perfume of hundreds of potted orange trees carried up from the Orangerie.

Not one for parties, Armand had kept strictly to the business he'd been assigned, until the man he was supposed to be keeping an eye on had disappeared behind closed chamber doors with a bevy of beauties tucked under his lace-cuffed arms. Wasn't much to do after that, save down a few goblets of wine and resign himself to the festive mood. Armand's duties did not include reporting on inner-bedroom antics.

Threading his fingers up through the luxuriously fluid coils of his seductress's hair, Armand coaxed his willing captive closer.

Er—no. On second thought, it was *he* that had been captured by *her*. Such novelty!

Curls as thick as his sword hilt slithered like snakes around his fingers. Armand was aware of her leg pressing between his thighs. A leg hampered by layers of abundant fabric. All the same, he was sure she could feel his arousal against her thigh, shrouded only by his velvet breeches.

Always one to defy discretion, Armand trailed his forefinger around her slender waist and up the boned bodice that squeezed her body in its clutches. As the violet silk ended, his fingers drew over the narrow lace ruffles of her chemise before touching flesh. She was full, hot, and wanting beneath his palm. The moment demanded he rip open the ribbons of her bodice and plunge his mouth against the sweet ripeness of her breasts.

And why the hell not? This masked vixen was ready and more than willing.

But as rapidly as she'd attached herself to him, his wicked playmate pulled away. Befuddled by the sudden detachment of her lips and loss of sultry, undulating flesh against his fingers, Armand managed a weak, drunken smile as his eyes lazily searched out hers.

Framed within the black-velvet mask shone two brilliant gemstones, limpid and fiery at the same time. Defiant. They seemed to say, "I shall do as I please."

And please her he would.

Her lips, burnished a deep crimson from her compelling kiss, parted into an O. "Pardon, Monsieur." Her dulcet voice was the very opposite of her kiss. Beneath her lowered nose curled a smile, not so much embarrassed as successful. "I thought you were someone else."

Flitting waves of lavender lace whispered across Armand's fingertips as she turned and dashed away from him and the festive notes of the Spanish imported *sarabande*. He grasped for a touch of the copper coils that bounced over her shoulders, but cupped only air in his fist. Trapped in a flabbergasted pose, Armand could not find his voice as he witnessed the woman's skirts disappear around a corner that led into the royal hunting lodge.

As he came to from his stupor, the woman's challenging

declaration worked to clear his senses as no morning-after could.

"Someone else?" Armand uttered. The Saint-Sylvestre pride—ingrained in all the men of his family—jerked him to alertness. *Someone else?* "We'll see about that!"

Taking chase, Armand darted down the aisle of Corinthian columns that lined the yellow-stone walls of the lodge just in time to see the woman's billowing skirts sail down the outer hallway. She paused outside a door, turned to cast him a teasingly wicked grin, then slipped from view.

"She thinks to play with Armand Saint-Sylvestre?" he said with a chuckle. "The woman does not know who she has chosen for sport. Coming, Mademoiselle Tease." He curved his hand around the befeathered brim of his beaver hat. "You cannot stoke the fire without expecting sparks."

The chamber door behind which she had disappeared was not locked. Nor had Armand expected it would be. Interesting, though. If this was her room, he was nothing but impressed. The hunting lodge wasn't large enough to house any more than the court. Himself, he had planned to spend the night in the stables.

Circumstances were starting to look up.

He elbowed the door and it opened with a creak. His masked Aphrodite stood across the room by the window, pushing the panes open to let in the summer breeze that wisped across the courtyard where she had just kissed him. Her crushed-plum skirts *swooshed* across the tiled floor. She did not turn to him as he approached, but showed no surprise when he turned her in his arms.

"But you make it too simple, Mademoiselle." The exotic scent of amber tempted him to nip the graceful curve of her jaw. She stiffened in his grip but did not make to struggle or call out. Yes, she still played the game.

"I warn you, Monsieur," she whispered, her voice husky

with only the satisfaction of the moment. "I—I am a dangerous woman."

Armand smiled at her stuttering declaration. There was a hint of doubt in that uncontrolled utterance. What sort of game did she play? And was she really as skilled as she hoped?

"I think you may very well be a lethal opponent, my goddess of seduction, but I"—he raised his face to look into her velvet-encircled eyes; bluer than any clear summer sky he'd ever stood in—"am up for the challenge."

Thinking to remove her mask, Armand lifted his hand. Her right brow, a copper arabesque placed by an artist on her face, arched expectantly above the black velvet.

He retracted his fingers. It would be far more intriguing to keep her identity a mystery. To debauch a nameless, masked woman? An exciting image in many a man's fantasies.

Sensing her relief in the subtle breath she blew through her nose, Armand countered, "For now, my lady. But should I win this game, your identity must be revealed to me."

"Fair enough."

This time *he* took control. She succumbed easily to the instruction of his kiss. Her body became liquid in his arms. her tenseness disappearing so that Armand had to support his purring kitten with both arms laced behind her back.

Wobbling backward, he sought out the high tester bed that he knew was just behind them. The backs of his calves hit against the walnut frame. His captive adjusted her weight— and pushed. Both landed on the bed in a tangle of seeking lips and groping arms.

Sweet temptation, she was his kind of woman! Ready, eager, and not a frail, shuddering virgin. He'd had enough of the weak, fan-fluttering *precieuses* who pranced about Paris in search of a husband. A husband who must steel his desires until after the marriage vows were said. For one must endure the proper *lengthy* engagement.

What man could wait months, sometimes a year, simply to

bed a woman? What was wrong with occasionally desiring a
brazen whore? No strings attached. Love them and walk away.

Armand rolled the woman onto her back. Unseen petticoats
whispered sweet promises, his own breath answering in winds
of desire. Paying heed to her inquisitive persimmon kisses, his
right hand slipped up to unlace her bodice. An echelon of satin
bows, so deeply violet they were almost black, slid over the
whorls of his fingers, each easily unfastened. Beneath the ribbons, the stays were unhooked with a few deft jerks. Success!

Her satisfied moan prompted him to seek out the hardened
bud of her breast with his tongue. The sensation of her finger-
nails driving across his scalp pushed Armand's self-control to
the limit. Damn the control, it was time to storm the Bastille!

Armand pressed his body the length of hers, grinding his
urgent need against her hip. By the eternal, this was too incredible to be real. He'd always had no trouble attracting the eye
of a beautiful woman, but never had one literally thrown herself
into his arms like this.

And he had every intention of taking full advantage of the
situation.

"Tell me your name," he rasped.

Beneath her skirts swirled layers of slippery petticoats, of
which Armand had to sort and scramble through to finally feel
the soft ribbon banding her stocking and, finally, the inviting
flesh of her thigh.

"Names are of no concern," she managed in gasps. "What
is important, is that I have succeeded in capturing my quarry.
The trap was set, and now 'tis full."

Armand smiled. My, but she was the confident one. But so
true, her declaration of triumph. Not that he minded being prey
to this enticing predator. "Now that you have captured me,
what are your intentions?"

Her eyes were as a cat's before the pounce, vibrant with the
knowledge of imminent success. "To devour you."

"Really?" His hand inched towards the softness between

her legs. She arched her back and moaned. "I beg to differ, it seems I am the one in control."

"Not . . ." She inhaled a deep breath—and screamed, "For long!"

Healthy set of lungs on this one. Wildly eager, too.

Armand bent down to push up her skirts. One layer of vexatious petticoats and another. And another. Billowing fabric ballooned this way and that, and settled upon his head.

A sharp *thwack* froze Armand in his pursuits, two layers of petticoats concealing his view of the room. It sounded like she'd knocked a chair leg hard against the floor. But they were on the bed. And the chairs were—

"Madeleine!"

The woman in whose skirts Armand had lost his hands and head bolted upright on the bed.

Armand jerked his head to alert. A gossamer layer of petticoats clung to his face. He blew at the material in an attempt to clear his vision.

The woman clutched her opened bodice together with one hand and grabbed Armand's lace-encircled wrist with the other. "Papa!"

"Papa?" Armand felt an acid swirl begin in his throat. He closed his eyes and clenched his jaw, his free hand quickly retreating from the soft delights of flesh and silk.

"Remove your hands from beneath my daughter's skirts, blackguard!" A powder-haired senior wobbled across the floor, his damask slippered feet shuffling, the bob stitched to the end of his nightcap bouncing against one hunched shoulder. "You wish to violate a young woman's virtue?"

"Tell me this is just a nightmare," Armand whispered, more to himself than anyone. He resisted hiding his head in her skirts. The sensuous shuffle of fabric no longer promised pleasure.

"I'll see to it 'tis done properly," the old man huffed, and reiterated with a clang of his cane across the bedpost.

"Papa!"

Armand slid off the bed and held placating hands before him, more to block the swing of the old man's cane than anything. "Monsieur, you do not understand, it was she—"

"Blast and damnation! You young rakes think you can have every skirt in Paris and not have to answer the consequences. The devil take your rapscallion ways! Simon!"

"No, Papa!"

So much for brazen whores. Armand cast *Madeleine* a quick look. Judging from Papa's rage she was most likely a virgin—

Wait.

A virgin? With her bedside manner?

"Where is Simon?" the old man bellowed, his cane poking the floor with every step.

Perplexed beyond all measure, Armand barely noticed the warm breeze that brushed his cheek. A sickening ache birthed in his gut. Never had he been caught in such a compromising situation. A . . . wait a minute . . . a breeze?

Breezes only came from windows. *Open* windows.

Armand cocked his head to the side, keeping one eye trained on the swinging cane, the other scanning his peripheral surroundings. Perhaps all was not lost. An expert at fast escapes, thanks to an illustrious past making quick escapes from widows' bedrooms, Armand backed toward the window, his hand on the sword hilt at his hip. He thought to draw it on the old man, but the decrepit senior had turned and taken to yelling down the hallway for Simon. Most likely a servant. Pray God, not a member of the king's guard.

Armand glanced toward the window, where a thin olive branch scratched lazily across the opened pane. He wasn't about to remain and face whatever consequences Papa had in mind. Papa? A lump the size of a rotten field melon formed below Armand's rib cage. This was not good at all. If he had ever become involved with a woman in the past, he'd been damned sure she was an orphan or a widow. No ties to anything. Save money.

Outside, the distant melody of violins and flutes decorated the night. Armand darted a careful glance to the woman on the bed. She clung to the bedpost, her cat's eyes no longer victorious. Instead, they frightfully waited Papa's return. A long curl of copper swirled across the soft dunes of her semiexposed décolletage.

Madeleine, eh?

Another time, Armand thought wistfully. *After the old man is dead and buried.*

"*Au revoir, mon amour,*" he called as he turned and jumped onto the window ledge, his leather boots scuffing across a frivolous piece of fringed drapery. His spurs jingled as he frantically fought to shake the material from his heel. Armand was thankful that his mystery woman had not led him upstairs above the ground floor. He jumped wide, but his sword caught the edge of the yew shrubbery queued beneath the window. He tumbled into a roll, inhaling murky water from a puddle that caught his fall.

Armand spit out the distasteful liquid. "*Spllaaa!*"

"*Arrêtez!*"

The point of a rapier greeted Armand just below his chin. And another to his chest, and another above his right ear.

He looked up into a half circle of blue livery, the king's household troops—fortunately not his own—each with rapiers drawn and aimed at body parts he would certainly like to preserve. No smiles beneath the red-plumed beaver hats. Not even a flinched brow.

"You don't understand," he started.

One of the men looked to the open window. "Is this the one?"

Armand cringed when the old man's voice instructed, "Bring the blackguard back inside. I've a priest waiting."

* * *

Left alone in her room while *Papa* saw that the *lecherous blackguard* was escorted inside, Madeleine quickly hooked up her stays and adjusted her skirts. She glanced into the etched mirror, fussed with her curls, and drew in a deep breath.

"I cannot believe you are doing this," her reflection chided.

"Yes, but I did it," Madeleine returned. *"Mon Dieu,* what have I done?" And knowing the reason she behaved so unlike herself, she quickly answered, "What that man has done!"

She pressed a palm to her breast to calm her racing heartbeats. The satin ribbons, which had done little to protect her body just moments ago, had been hastily retied and now spilled over her fingers in reckless disregard.

That man's hands had slid with wanton fervor across her flesh—like no man had ever done before. He'd taken her breast into his mouth! His hot, sweet mouth. An act that had sparked the most incredible feelings within her. Everywhere, she had tingled. Everywhere, she had wanted to be touched. How her muscles had clenched and relaxed and then tightened again at the new sensations.

It had been so easy to overlook her inhibitions. Not nearly as difficult as she had expected. For when she had kissed him in the courtyard all nervousness left. It was as though she were someone else. A someone else very comfortable initiating a kiss with a handsome man. A man whose touch had transformed her. Changed her into a desirable, beautiful woman. Madeleine had given herself up to the moment, her mind knowing she should not, while her heart screamed yes, yes, and yes!

And his lust-heavy whispers—oh, his deep syrupy voice—had sent knee-bending shivers throughout her body. By all that had ever been sacred, if she had known that a man's voice could do such things to her—she might have kissed one long ago!

Ah, but she had received that one kiss. Chaste and dry. On her wedding night.

But that was in the past. The future—even as controlled as she had allowed it to become—promised decadent delights indeed.

"I certainly hope I can complete my task without . . . well . . . without falling in love."

Combing through her loose hair, Madeleine focused blindly on the mirror. Love would only hinder the part she had been cast to play. Reason told her she must remain impartial. Never forget the ultimate goal. But at the same time, the act of love was a definite requirement. At least on Monsieur Saint-Sylvestre's part.

He struggled, but the three guardsmen holding him by arms, shoulders, and ankle were determined. "This is preposterous!" Armand declared to anyone who would listen. "You are taking this much too far. The woman is not some untouched maiden. She seduced *me!*"

The men's chuckles succeeded in humiliating Armand even further. Had he just admitted to being seduced? He, Armand Saint-Sylvestre, great pretender that he had been? *He* was supposed to be the seducer. Pretty young widows beware, for when Armand Saint-Sylvestre crosses your path, resistance is futile. Armand could smell a recent widow leagues away and through a thick spring fog. She would succumb to his desires at the wink of his eye, and never even notice the missed jewels and coin.

Charm had been his weapon, a steel-encased heart his armor.

Now here he stood, shackled on either side by laughing ruffians. And standing before him, his hair tousled after being roused from sleep, and holding a Bible, was the mysterious Simon le Beuvier. A priest!

The man known to Armand only as Papa stood next to him,

his eyes, fringed by a frothy hedgehog wig, fixed on Armand. Great masses of white hair sprouted from his eyebrows, and his chin as well. Wasn't much Armand could see on the old man's face, save the glitter in his eyes.

"No one toys with my daughter's virtue." Papa stomped the ground with his cane. "I'll make an honest man of you, then you may have the prize you so desperately sought."

"But I don't want—" Armand choked off his retort as the cane—seeming to work more of its own volition than at that of its owner—stabbed him in the chest. "This is insane! Your daughter does not want this. She does not even know me. Or my name! Ask her yourself."

"I shall. Madeleine!"

The woman in question suddenly appeared at Armand's side. She had rehooked her bodice and fastened her tousled curls upon her head with a length of violet ribbon. The velvet mask was nowhere in sight.

Armand felt his heart catch just below his neck. God above, but she was beautiful. Her skin was as fine as porcelain, and her lips, still burnished from his kiss, were like the petals of a deep summer rose. Her face was a dream—an elusive image he chased through the night.

But when he tried to make eye contact, she only bowed to her father.

"Was this man trying to take advantage of your virtue?"

She nodded, her lower lip thrust out for added effect.

"What?" Armand tried to wrench his arm from his captors' hold, but was unsuccessful. "It was she who kissed me!"

Papa ignored Armand's tirade; instead he lifted his daughter's chin with hands completely covered by the lace edging his sleeves. "You know I don't approve of such relations out of wedlock."

She nodded again, still not looking to Armand.

"Do you love this man?"

Now the truth would be told. Armand bent before Madeleine, trying to catch her elusive gaze.

She nodded again.

"What? Love? Mademoiselle, I've known you all of ten minutes. This entire situation is beyond reason. You do not even know—. What is my name? Tell me that!"

Finally, she brought her gaze up to explore his. Copper lashes dusted above her pale cheeks, but the defiance had returned to her eyes. "Armand Saint-Sylvestre."

Shocked to hear his own name cross her passion-swollen lips, Armand could only stand stiffly, his jaw cocked wide, his gaze fixed on the glittering triumph in her eyes. Had he mentioned his name to her in the heat of passion? No . . . he didn't recall doing so. Of course, he'd lost count after the sixth goblet of wine as well . . .

"You see?" The old man tapped the priest's Bible with his cane. "Marry them."

And the ceremony began. Words spoken in Latin registered as cloudy nonsense in the back of Armand's mind. Comprehension completely left. Only the pain of dispassionate fingers gripping his upper arms registered tenfold, weakening his resistance and utterly consigning Armand to stand a blind and mute recipient of fate's most ridiculous of punishments. Until—

"Do you take this man to be your husband?"

"I will," Madeleine answered strongly, without so much as a glance Armand's way.

"And you, Monsieur Saint-Sylvestre—"

"No!" Armand stomped his boot and craned his head into Madeleine's personal space, forcing her to look at him. "My name. How did you—"

Papa's cane pressed against Armand's neck, causing him to swallow mid-word. "You *do* take this woman."

"This is madness." Armand conveyed his desperation in drawn-out syllables. "I will not. You do not even know who

I am. I could be a devious blackguard. A cur! A despicable criminal!''

The old man did not waver. His gray eyes shone brightly, more vivid than Armand had ever seen for a man of advanced age.

As each second ticked by, the cane pressed deeper into his flesh. Still held from behind, Armand could not move away. Nor did the guards who held him show any sign of compassion. As well they should not. To the snickering guardsmen, he was just another nameless rogue caught with his breeches down.

If only he could reveal his alliances to one of the king's closest advisors. That would put an abrupt end to this fiasco. Unfortunately, he had been sworn to silence.

"I know," Papa said in firm beats, "that in exchange for the debauchery you so desire you will keep my daughter and care for her and treat her justly. For I have the king's ear, my son."

The king's ear, indeed. Armand gagged. Papa wrenched his cane away from his neck.

Madeleine cleared her throat. "Please," her ruby lips mouthed to Armand.

Eyes as clear and priceless as the fine jewels he'd once stolen to feed his family pleaded with him. No, they *begged* him. She wanted this marriage for reasons beyond Armand's comprehension. She *needed* him.

But why?

Her smile threatened to wilt. She was beautiful, exotic, and desirable. Her scent filled Armand's senses. Sweet perfume of rare amber. Damn, if only he hadn't the taste of her on his tongue! For if there were anything that weakened his resolve 'twas a saucy smile and the taste of pleasures yet to come.

"I cannot believe this is happening."

"I shall ensure you do not regret this," she said. But her smile was not saucy now; it had wilted to a desperate moue. "Help me?"

"No."

"Please." She slinked closer, caging his legs in with her wide skirts. "Do this for me." She pleaded very quietly, her implied desperation speaking louder than her voice. "I need your help."

Words like that, and issued in such a devastating plea, pierced the steel armor and seared Armand's heart. *Tap, tap.*

Had he just heard someone tapping? Odd.

Ah, but what kind of help did this fiery-crowned vixen need? And why, of all the men at Versailles tonight, must it be him?

He swallowed again. He had wanted her to meet his gaze before, but now she did not waver, and he'd be damned if those vexatious cat's eyes had taken on a new innocence.

They were all innocent!

But none of the victims from his past had ever had soft copper curls. Or such a pale, ethereal face, like that of a treasured porcelain doll. And the teardrop that threatened to spill from her eye . . .

Damn it all to a frost covered hell, he'd lost this one!

"And if I help you," he said in equally low tones, his palm smoothing over the hilt of his sword, "what will you do for me?"

"Anything."

Armand quirked a brow.

Anything covered quite a lot of ground. Most particularly it could be construed as a promise of debauchery. But was one night's passion worth the saying of vows? And what of tomorrow morning? Weren't vows spoken with the intention of forever?

"Monsieur?"

The touch of her forefinger to his chin was like a butterfly landing on rusted armor. Armand's senses were clouded, he'd not been thinking straight since she'd first plunged into his arms. Though for all he'd imbibed earlier, he was dead sober now.

Vows? Forever? "Impossible!"

"I promise you won't regret such kindness." Her breath teased his lips with a warm tickle. "Say yes now. I shall explain later."

"Anything, eh?"

She nodded and mouthed the word. *Anything.* And it entered his thoughts on silken waves of song. *Anything . . . anything . . .*

Ah hell!

"Very . . ." Armand choked on the word, but finally spit it out, ". . . well."

The cane fell to the ground with a hollow clatter. Papa clutched his chest.

Madeleine rushed to her father. "He is in pain!"

The priest shouted over the sudden commotion, "Do you take this woman?"

"Uh . . ." Armand gauged the climactic scene before him, his vision also scanning the grounds about him. Escape was a quick jump over a trimmed yew hedge, a dash across an empty courtyard, and a full-speed race to the surrounding forest, where he could lose his accusers under the starless blanket of midnight.

Papa sputtered and gasped, his fingers grasping blindly through the air. Armand was still held by two men.

"Do you take this woman?"

Freedom so close made the priest easy to ignore.

"Quickly!" Madeleine cried. Her eyes caught Armand's and he could see—no—*feel* her terror. It resonated in his breast like ripples on a pond, tight circles of pain echoing outward. "Say I will," she pleaded.

Armand swallowed. His arms tensed as he gripped his fingers into fists. Papa heaved and choked for air. Another minute, and the old man might be dead. Armand would be free. But . . . He could see the trail the teardrop had painted down Madeleine's cheek. *So real her pain.*

Armand sighed and released his fists. "Damn it anyway, I will!"

His captors released him and rushed to catch the old man as he collapsed. Madeleine cried out. Armand looked over Papa's face. Still. Deathlike. In a moment of desperation he had wished for Papa's death earlier when he had only thoughts of debauchery in mind, but he'd not thought anyone would take him literally. "Is he dead?"

"No," Madeleine whispered as she stood. "He's just fainted. Papa is very ill. He . . . he needs rest."

The priest cleared his throat and snapped his Bible shut, quite oblivious to the entire debacle as he sleepily declared, "You may now kiss the bride."

Kiss the bride?

Armand looked to Madeleine. But of course. Freedom was already lost, why not claim the consolation prize?

The sparkle returned to her eyes. It seemed they stood alone amidst the confusion. No sound, save the beat of his heart, intruded. Actions and commotion were but a fuzzy backdrop to the passion that vied to pull the two together. Armand leaned across Papa's inert body, ready to kiss—

"Huurrummph!" Papa miraculously jerked awake. "You've already had enough of that!"

Two

What had just happened? By the darkest evils, how had he allowed some lustful female and a crotchety old man to force him into marriage?

No, no, Armand knew what had happened. It was that promise of *anything* that had blurred his thinking and redirected his thoughts down to his loins.

He pressed a finger to his brow. His scalp felt tight, as if a wooden torture device were stretched from ear to ear. And somebody was still twisting!

The hallway in the south wing of the hunting lodge echoed his pacing footsteps; his spurs clanked dully upon the marble floor; his right fist pounded his thigh. Papa had been carried away, the priest mumbling unintelligible Latin over the old man's chest. Still alive.

Unfortunately.

This game the woman and her father played read like a ploy he would have devised years ago. A plot planned and carried out by him in search of riches to support his family. But the entire Saint-Sylvestre clan was now self-supporting. No longer did his brothers and sister need a highwayman's booty to survive.

Determined to become an honest man, Armand had meant every word of his promise to leave the criminal life behind in hopes of gaining a commission in the king's household troops. It was high time he polished his image and started living the upright life. Either that or face a swing on the gallows.

For a year now he'd served the crown in a minor foot troop. Miserable work for a man accustomed to independence and a modicum of clean. As for the pay, well, a month's wages barely put food on his table. But a *half* month's wages was ridiculous. He'd lost weight this last year—if not the fire that had once lit the pride in his eyes. Armand could not continue on such rations.

But the captain of the guards would not allow him to join the household ranks—a higher-paying, more elite troop of musketeers—until he'd proven his loyalty to the crown. Armand was, after all, a former criminal. Trust must be earned. Luckily, Captain Lambert knew Monsieur Colbert. The finance minister sought a man with a background similar to Armand's. He needed someone who could ease himself into a precarious situation and walk undaunted before the enemy without fear of discovery. Colbert required a spy.

Armand had been more than obliging to step back into the adventure and intrigue that had become like blood in his veins over the last decade.

He craved the challenge, the action . . . the fire.

His assignment? To secure evidence that would prove Nicholas Fouquet, the Superintendent of Finances, had been embezzling money from the king's coffers. A rather difficult task thus far, considering Fouquet was quite well loved by each and every person with whom he came in contact. The man wielded charm with the same practiced skill as Armand had when he'd been eyeing a widow's sizable purse.

But Armand had one advantage. It took one pretender to know another. And Fouquet wasn't fooling Armand.

Soon, he would have the evidence Colbert needed either to clear the financier of his suspected crimes or else put him away for the rest of his days. From then on, his loyalties proven, Armand's future could only improve. Life promised to become better every day.

Until Armand had allowed himself to be tempted by a woman's kiss. And those pleading eyes. That had been his downfall, to look into Madeleine's eyes and recognize the fear that had once lived in his own heart. For one moment he had known her dread, and had wanted to chase it away.

But actually to agree to the marriage?

Damn the wine he'd drunk. For surely, if he would have been connected in the least to his wits, he'd have escaped and fled before the priest had even cracked the Bible.

Hell, what was he doing, trying to blame the wine? It was Armand's own fault he now found himself in a duo instead of the single form he preferred.

"I cannot have a wife. I do not need a wife." He stopped mid-pace and worked his forefinger over his mustache, tracing it down the side of his mouth to the smudge of beard that always resisted the razor. "What shall I *do* with a wife?"

Very well, so he could imagine a few earthly delights he might like to explore with the assistance of a wife. To finish their earlier tryst first came to mind. It had been much too long since he'd drawn his hands up the bare flesh of a woman's thigh. Far too long since he'd nuzzled his face in a delicious meadow of bosom and woman-scent and thrilled to the hum of her satisfied cries.

"Foolishness. I don't even know the woman . . ."

Though, she was very lovely. Flawless complexion, lightly powdered perhaps, but boasting of the smooth surface of creamy Italian marble. Definitely to his taste.

"Don't even consider . . ."

Long, rich hair of sun-burnished copper highlighted with a deeper shade that glinted like shards of garnet, each curl so lush and wide that he could lose his fingers within the thick columns.

"She has promised *anything* . . ."

Wide, expressive eyes, glass cut and colored lapis lazuli, like a section from one of the rose windows of Nôtre Dame.

"Mm, yes." His senses overtook logic, forcing away further mental argument.

Delicious kisses, flavored with persimmon and a sigh. Impossible to believe that she still possessed her virtue when she commanded a man's carnal desires with a mere kiss. But as her father had said . . .

"Damnation!" Armand kicked the wall. An iron candelabra rattled near his shoulder. He pressed his forehead to the ornate burned-velvet paper that coated the halls of the palace. It pained him to think. Why had he even come to the fête tonight? To catch a glimpse of Louise de la Valliere, the king's new mistress? All of Paris had fallen in love with her charm and grace. No, he'd been following Fouquet's every move; and it was the financier who had eyes for la Valliere when the king had her not in his grasp.

Zut alors! A hell of a lot of spying Armand had been doing with his hands up a woman's skirts.

Colbert must not hear of this. Nor Captain Lambert. He'd have to remedy the situation before dawn. Fouquet returned to the Louvre tomorrow, and Armand must be on his heels.

He had gotten himself into a tricky situation. There was only one thing a man of his nature could do.

"The woman likes to play games? I can play games, too."

She did not see her conflicted emotions flickering across a carefully powdered complexion. Instead, images of a sweet cooing babe appeared in the wide silvered glass set into the gold fastenings upon the vanity.

"I do this for you, Stephan," Madeleine whispered, sniffing away a sudden tear.

Less than a week ago Madeleine's cousin, Valérie Déscouvertes, baroness of Mononfête, had sent word requesting a visit from her lifelong friend. Stricken to find her cousin wasting away in bed, Madeleine had sat quietly with Valérie.

There were many factors that had led to Valérie's failing health. Newly widowed and left with the baron's gambling debts, the Déscouvertes's Marais estate was slowly being picked clean by creditors. Pregnancy had reduced her sunny demeanor to a sallow, tired lump. Then there was the brief affair she'd had after the baron's death.

Madeleine knew Valérie had been seduced by an idler, then left without a word.

"I want you to promise you'll be Stephan's guardian when I am gone," Valerie had said. She touched Madeleine's wrist with her cold hand, and at that very moment, Madeleine had known her friend was dying. "More than a guardian. He'll need . . . a mother."

Slipping her fingers through Valérie's hand, Madeleine had brought it to her lips and kissed the cool flesh.

"Your inheritance should see Stephan through. It was fortunate Pierre left you so much. I feel absolutely beaten with the creditors marching in and out, day after day, with yet another piece of my life."

Yes, so great a fortune Madeleine had inherited. But for how long could she retain it?

When Valérie had tired, Madeleine had walked out behind two rugged bill collectors carting out the household silver and right into Valérie's uncle, Nicholas Fouquet, master of finances and charmer of patrons. All who left his presence strolled away glitter-eyed and enamored. He boasted of affairs with two of the court's most lovely women and shared the ear of foreign dignitaries, as well as their wives' eager glances.

"I understand you've agreed to become guardian to the child after my niece takes her final breath," he said to her back as Madeleine struggled to compose the storm of emotions that battled inside her head.

"Indeed."

"A single woman without trade or husband to assist?"

"I've the finances to ensure Stephan is raised with everything he should ever need."

"The finances. Ah yes . . ." The click of Fouquet's heels on the marble floor screamed inside Madeleine's head as he sashayed around her skirts and clutched her hands. "For the *moment* you've the finances."

"What do you mean by that?"

He studied her face, his thin, pursed lips seeming to pause for some sort of grand effect, then smartly announced, "Paul de Pellison is my secretary."

The name sent shivers of dread scrambling through Madeleine's veins.

Madeleine quickly learned that Fouquet needed her assistance. He suspected he was being followed by one of the king's men and needed to plant a spy in his path. And if there were any chance she could make the man fall in love with her, all the better.

Why? Fouquet would not divulge his reasons, only he made it obvious that her life would be hell if she did not comply.

When she had protested lack of skill, the financier claimed Madeleine could make any man fall in love with her. She was so easy with people, charming them with a smile and her gracious manner. And she had been married, after all, so her virtue would not risk further tarnishing should the scenario lend itself to such action.

To that, Madeleine had clamped her mouth shut. She walked

a fine line with Nicolas Fouquet. He could not know the entirety
of her struggles with Paul de Pellison. But she couldn't be sure.

That damned marriage!

Yes, she had once been wed. For an exceedingly short time.
Not for love, but for security. Of course, Pierre de Pellison had
not had forever in mind when his heart had ceased to beat on
the eve of their wedding night.

Thanks to her mother's stipulations regarding the marriage
contract, Madeleine was now comfortably settled in the Marais,
not far from Valérie's home, with enough income to see her
to death. And to ensure Stephan's future.

Until Fouquet had sashayed into her life.

But to seduce a man into loving her? How could she possibly
achieve such a thing? She had no more experience with men
beyond the actors she had known while serving a short stint
in Molière's troop after Pierre's death. All had treated her as
a daughter, save Molière, whose blatant advances had cornered
Madeleine on more than one occasion.

Ah, but it was a hideous bargain Madeleine had hastily agreed
to.

"He is a spy," Fouquet had said as he'd escorted her from
Valérie's home. "I'll not tolerate spies in the king's court.
There are also rumors that he was once a highwayman who
specifically sought out widows as his prey. Be cautious, for
our spy is skilled. And remember, if you wish a man to spill
his deepest secrets, you must become a trusted ally. No man
trusts a woman that has not bared her flesh before him and
taken him into her bed."

How fortunate—as she was determined to find some fortune
in this affair she'd been blackmailed into—the man Fouquet
requested she seduce was so handsome. And very adept at
kissing. It would make her part much easier to perform.

But a performance this charade must remain. The finest
actress never allowed the characters she portrayed to seep into
her life after the curtain fell. And so Madeleine would play her

part, and play it well, and then strip away the costume and
leave the story—and the man—behind.

Oh hell. She caught her chin in her cupped palms. She was
eager to dive into this charade. What she had missed on her
wedding night, pined for release now. Love Pierre, she had
not. Nor had he ever expressed the same to her, for theirs had
been an arranged marriage. Truly, Madeleine had given up
hope of ever knowing the passion a woman could experience.

Until she had kissed the spy with the masterful hands and
hypnotic voice.

Her chamber door creaked open. Madeleine looked into the
mirror. Lucid umber eyes held her gaze, stirring within her a
mutinous need to surrender. Armand Saint-Sylvestre spoke of
his intentions with his eyes. And such intentions were not of
sweet kisses to her cheek and a night wished well and alone.

And so, Act Two must begin.

Three

"Monsieur, I believe you are mistaken. This is my room."

He pushed the door shut and tossed his plumed hat across the room, where it landed with rehearsed flair on the tester bed. "Ours, I believe, Madame. Are we not husband and wife?"

Madeleine stood and turned to face his devilish smile. Fouquet had warned her of this man's rumored charm, of his ability to play a role with the ease of much practice. But she could have never imagined her prey to be quite so ... fascinating.

"We—we are—I am, your wife," she stuttered.

Armand eased onto the feather bed and crossed one long leg over the other. Deep burgundy velvet fashioned his breeches and doublet, long slashes from shoulder to elbow revealed a pristine white shirt. A cavalier. Fitting dress for a man who wished to blend with the exotic peacocks at court. Though Fouquet had also informed her that Saint-Sylvestre had supposedly left pretending behind; reports from the Louvre said he had garnered a commission in a foot regiment.

If the man knew so much about Armand's past, how then

could he possibly need a spy? That thought began to perplex, when the spurs on Armand's boot clicked against the walnut bed frame, bringing her attention back to the fore.

"Then this is my room, Madame Saint-Sylvestre. A woman whose virtue—which, I must say, still remains in question—"

"How dare you!"

He raised a finger. "Ah, ah. You must grant me the benefit of the doubt after falling victim to your brazen seductions."

Madeleine bit her lip before a sharp retort could jump out unguarded. She *had* performed gloriously. Why, she'd shocked even herself with the ease with which she'd taken to her character.

"You set your traps well, Madeleine. So tell me, are you pleased with your prize?"

She defended herself without a bit of hesitation. "I did not plan for Papa to appear." Though why Paul de Pellison—the very man she wished to distance herself from—had been chosen to play Papa vexed her to no end. Perhaps Fouquet's irritating way of keeping her under thumb and reminding her of what she could lose?

"Really? You would have me believe that Papa was not waiting outside your chamber door in hopes of snagging a husband for his dowerless daughter?"

"Dowerless?"

"I can only guess," he said with a dismissive gesture. "How else would Papa ever secure a future for his daughter? Alas," Armand continued, "the two of you have failed. I am but a penniless rogue. The king's guards will not have me, but as a miserable foot soldier, for I am not skilled in trade or labor. All my life I have lived off my wits and the kindness of others. How do you expect that I shall support a wife?"

The kindness of others? When she knew his favorite victim had been widows? How dare he! "I'm sure you'll find a means to support a family."

"Family? Ha! I do not think so." He uncrossed his legs and

stood tall. A sinister shadow fell over his eyes and coated his words as well. A cocoon of candle glow surrounded the two of them, as if in a bubble of light. "I haven't figured out what your game is, Madame Tease, but I've decided to call your bluff."

She raised a brow. He approached slowly. A flash of danger flared in Madeleine's breast. *Flee,* her conscience whispered. *Yes, escape while you can,* her mind agreed. But her body demanded she stand firm.

"Now . . ." He gripped her shoulders and walked her backward until her thighs connected with the ornate rosewood boiserie set into the wall. "It is my turn." Swift fingers danced over her bodice, untying the satin bows for the second time tonight. "You promised me anything in return for a positive answer to our wedding vows."

Madeleine gripped his hands, momentarily stalling his hurried actions. "You needn't be so rough. I may be willing to sacrifice—"

"Sacrifice?" The top ribbon zipped through the silk-thread grommets with a smart jerk of his hand. Armand turned and waved the ribbon like a victory flag above his head. Then he snapped before her, catching her gaze in his steady eyes, not allowing her to look aside, for he dodged to match her movements. "Why don't you let down this front, eh? If you confess now—"

"I've nothing to confess," she countered with as much command as possible.

Two hot fingers sneaked between her loosened bodice and breasts. A sigh rose in Madeleine's throat. What his touch did to her willpower!

"We can have the marriage annulled and each walk our own way. No harm done, save a night spent fulfilling the requirements of *anything.*"

Annulment. The word was not at all a surprise. Fortunately

for her nerves, she and Fouquet had scripted this scene. And she never forgot a line.

"But of course, Monsieur. We know naught of one another. 'Tis foolish. Although . . ." She bowed her head and pressed her fingers over his, which now toyed with the second bow.

"Although?"

"It is Papa." She glanced aside and closed her eyes. *Think tragedy, Madeleine. Think of what Paul de Pellison could do with the truth.* "He's in such a dreadful state. You saw for yourself his wheezing and inability to walk without a cane. And his attacks! I fear upsetting him further."

Armand heaved a defeated sigh and slipped his hands from her bodice. Signs of compliance? Madeleine counted on it.

"The surgeon said it was his heart." She looked to Armand, pleased to see that he appeared worried. Or was it annoyance that tightened his jaw? "Perhaps the annulment can be delayed until Papa has improved?"

Or until she had fulfilled her duties to Fouquet.

Armand appeared to savor her suggestion for a moment, rubbing his thumb and forefinger over his chin. His dark eyes trailed the length of the stone floor.

"Oh please—" She halted at the abrupt flip of his hand before her face.

"Just stop it," he hissed, his eyes trained on the floor.

"But—"

"Don't do that!"

"Do what?" she said on a well-conjured sniffle. "I am doing nothing, Monsieur, but standing here . . . feeling rather . . ." *Sniff.* ". . . sad."

"Exactly!"

"Exactly what?"

"That is exactly what you are doing." He began to pace before her in curt military style. "You do the feeling-rather-sad thing well, you know that?"

He was good. But she was better. "Monsieur, do you accuse me of—of acting?"

He stopped pacing, turned to her, and quirked a dark brow. How delicious could a human being look with such a simple gesture? Madeleine felt her heart begin to ooze between her ribs.

"I only wish to keep Papa from further upsetting himself. Please, Monsieur, if you could but see it in your heart to grant me a few days. Perhaps a week."

"A week?"

"No more," she countered to his angry bark. "I swear. I feel sure within a week Papa will improve. I've a notion to have him brought to Les Invalides tomorrow morning. The military hospital can provide him the best care possible; it is new and quite clean. If he should not improve, well . . ."

Never had she felt such precise scrutiny of her face until this moment. The man traced her eyes, touched them with his gaze, prying deep within to seek the truth. Would he find what he was looking for? Was this the same look he had used to read his victims before seducing them into his arms?

Armand swiped a defeated fist through the air. "You don't want this marriage any more than I do. That is correct?"

She shrugged and looked away, only to have him jerk her chin and her eyes back into his cage of vision. "You do not, Madame, I can see it in your reluctance."

"I only wish Papa to leave this world knowing his daughter was married and happy."

"Happy? That's the sort of happiness the old man wants, is for his daughter to be forced into marriage with a stranger?"

"Please. Papa needs to know I will not be left on my own. He will not know what happens when he is—should he . . . pass. You may have your annulment then."

He studied her for the longest time. He did not trust her. One falter to her stare, and he would know that Madeleine was not being truthful. But something, that tiny flinch in his left eye, wanted to believe her.

And that was all she needed, a moment of doubt, of wanting to believe.

"Very well. Let it not be said Armand Saint-Sylvestre isn't a formidable opponent. I shall remain with you until the old coot has recovered sufficiently to withstand the news that you refuse this alliance, or . . . until he is dead. . . . But!"

Madeleine flinched at the deep declaration. She had expected a *but*. She'd stepped into smoldering ash when agreeing to Fouquet's request, knowing from that point on any move she made would only flame the embers. The trick would be to keep those embers from becoming a raging fire.

"There was mention of *anything*"

"I do recall saying that, Monsieur." She also recalled that had not been part of the script. Mention of *anything* had been a moment of panic on her part. "What might your definition of the term be?"

Armand walked toward the bed, hands crossed in front of him, his spurs jangling with each step. He plopped onto the thick, feather-stuffed mattress and patted the velvet counterpane.

Madeleine studied her opponent's actions. They both played a game. Though she had the advantage of knowing exactly what she wanted. She would serve Fouquet his information, and at the same time, enjoy the passion her body craved.

But could she feed that craving so soon? Yes, she wanted this man. And yes, she believed making love to him a requirement to discovering his secrets, as Fouquet had explained. But to be standing here now, so close to making love to a stranger, suddenly frightened her more than a thousand Nicolas Fouquets. She had to stall. To get her wits about her.

"Monsieur, if we have both already agreed to an annulment, I fear my loss of virtue may destroy all hope of ending the marriage."

"One's virtue is a difficult commodity to prove."

"But there are tests!"

"Really?"

Oh hell, where had that come from? She fingered the empty eyelet from which the slick violet ribbon had been claimed by her new husband. If there *were* tests, she hoped only to fail.

"Tests or not, I am quite unprepared to submit to such a request." Tonight. Although, tomorrow was another day.

"You said anything, and I intend to take you at your word, Madame Saint-Sylvestre. For as long as we are husband and wife you shall serve me exactly as a wife should. When I want. How I want. You shall submit."

This man's challenge set her blood to a slow and heavy drift within her veins. His regard made her feel molten and desirous. Beautiful. The flavor of her new husband's kisses still lingered in her mouth. Piquant and demanding.

The fingers smoothing across his smartly bearded jaw reminded her of the masterful caresses they had given her breasts as they lay upon this very bed just one hour ago. It wasn't difficult for her body to confess it wanted more. Much more. But she must bide her time. Submission would come. But only when she was ready.

Seduce and tease, Fouquet had coached. *That is how a spy operates, that is how you must work.*

Perhaps a little foreplay might cool his desires and satisfy him for the night. A sign of good faith?

Her opponent drew his eyes up her body and stopped where Madeleine had begun to trace the next ribbon in slow design with her forefinger. Such hungry scrutiny in his dark gaze.

"Submit? I—I'm not sure," she stuttered carefully, thinking her lines through before voicing them. "Perhaps . . . if we worked slowly toward the completion of our agreement?"

"Just how slow did you have in mind?"

Oh, hours and days and weeks of long and deep kisses, for sure.

Madeleine snapped out of her wandering thoughts, recalling

the last of Fouquet's requests. No, it had been more a warning. *Do not allow yourself to fall into his trap of seduction.*

"A few days? I promise you, Monsieur, I shall fulfill my obligations. Just . . . slowly. There are advantages to taking one's time."

He considered her offer without removing his eyes from hers. Divining the truth of her promises with his penetrating, all-seeing gaze. In a moment of pure abandon, Madeleine drew on the man's lusty power and flashed back at him her own sloe-eyed assurance that she was a woman of her word.

She wanted to be. She *would* be.

Maybe?

"Very well, I shall not take your virtue. For now."

A relieved sigh pushed from her mouth. She had won this round.

"But there are other ways to satisfy a man."

Madeleine certainly hoped so. The idea of not getting to at least taste the brew of seduction and passion simmering in his eyes was beyond consideration.

"And so, I must insist you undress for me."

"But you just said—"

His raised finger shortened her protest. "Don't you want to play my bluff?"

Well certainly, but . . . undress?

Relax, Madeleine, get control of yourself. Think!

She had revealed far more of her soul standing on a stage before hundreds. It should be easy enough to keep hold of her most valued secrets alone in a room lit by only one candle, and with only one man. She did wish a taste. And most certainly she must allow him the fantasy of having the upper hand.

Become the character.

Yes, she had come this far on courage alone, she would not flee now.

Madeleine turned and blew out the candle on the bedside vanity. The myriad of candles still glittering in the gardens shone through the window as if summer fireworks spread across the floor and highlighted half of the bed—the half her challenger lay upon.

"Do you need assistance?"

"I shouldn't think so," she drawled, quite unaware of what she was saying, for she could not tear her eyes from his intense gaze.

The bed ropes creaked as Armand leaned back on his elbows, the action parting his unbuttoned doublet and shirt to reveal a tuft of dark hair on his chest. As Madeleine tugged the second bow free she scrutinized his attire, feeling it much safer than lingering in his stare. Lace flowed around his wrist, not so wide as to be foppish, but enough there to prove his subtle vanity.

The second bow slipped from the silk-stitched eyelet, further parting her stays. By now she did not realize her actions had quickened. The third and final ribbon whispered to the floor. Her breasts felt tumid and warm.

Vulnerability threatening her composure, Madeleine directed her gaze at Armand's boots as she slipped the bone-stiffened bodice from her arms. His raven-dark boots were polished to a gloss. Further proof of his vanity, yet also a sign of care and precision. If she were to let down her guard for one moment, he would see through the charade.

"Madame?"

"What?" she asked without looking up. Her bodice ribbons lay in a swirl at her feet. Had she really done that? She clasped her hands before her breasts, sensing the rise in her body temperature through the thin gauze chemise.

"You are staring at my boots."

"Er, um . . . exceedingly fine craftsmanship."

"No, no." He rose in a breath, and tilted her chin up, stilling her with his hungry, exotic gaze. "Right here." He pointed to his eyes. "This is where you belong." The light of the candles glinted in each of his eyes.

Yes, indeed, what a delicious place to belong.

"Your seduction skills are waning from your garden kiss, Madame. Is it that you have changed your mind regarding the position you now find yourself in? We've already agreed to take things slowly. I give you my word I shall honor that agreement as long as I can trust you shall eventually fulfill said terms of *anything*."

She stepped back defiantly. Her flesh tingled beneath the sheer gauze chemise. But she did not balk. Something inside urged her on. Madeleine straightened her shoulders, drawing in a deep breath of the citrus-scented air from outside her window. The actress within wanted to perform, to be admired by the audience. "Does it look like I've changed my mind?"

Eyes focused on her like a bull preparing for the charge, his shoulder-length curly hair framing his masculine countenance, Armand stepped forward. His scent intoxicated her. Who would have thought a man could tempt without even touching? Why, the very smell of him, feral and masculine, made her want to reach out and pull him close. But at the same time his presence overwhelmed. She felt like a very small flower standing in the shadow of a great tree. He could choose either to shelter her with his shade or to suck the very life out from under her.

"You've the loveliest skin. So pale and creamy. Are you sure you are not a doll? A treasure sought by collectors?"

A trill of laughter bubbled across Madeleine's lips. "Monsieur, you are silly."

"Ahh . . . I like the sound of your voice when it is free and unguarded."

The heat of his knuckles brushed her waist. Madeleine stepped away from the sudden intensity of his nearness. "You are too close."

"Not nearly as close as you deemed earlier. I do believe it was you that pressed your lips to mine. Am I correct?"

"M-must I answer the obvious?" She stumbled and could move no further. Her shoulders connected with the velvet paper on the wall behind her. "I thought you had wanted me to merely undress? You seem rather anxious to explore territory that I fear may lead you away from the rules of the game.''

"Hunger has nothing to do with being anxious," he purred in a deep tone that rippled through her being and loosened her reflexive urge to push him away.

Hunger? Ah yes, the same hunger that gnawed at her own insides. A hunger that swirled in her womb and tingled through her groin. A new sensation that she wanted to answer, to feed. The small taste she'd been granted earlier had only whetted her appetite.

"I am hungry for this," he said as he cupped one breast in his hand.

Madeleine moaned, and then froze when she realized she had just moaned. So wanton she sounded!

His hand circled her breast and zoned in on the hardened nub in the center. She bit her lip and closed her eyes. She sensed his desire—hot and dark and needy.

"And I am hungry for this." He reached around her hip and ripped the loosened laces free, pulled her skirts and petticoats down, and pressed his hand to the tingling warmth of her stomach. Though her chemise remained, he claimed her as his own with such intimate caresses.

Madeleine allowed the shock to shudder through her, but by the time it reached her breasts, the sharp twinge had turned to what could only be desire. Her entire body quivered in anticipation of his next move.

"I think we've gone far enough for tonight, don't you, Monsieur?"

"I have only just begun."

His words seemed to have been drawn from the very loins Madeleine sought to protect herself from. The true meaning of temptation made itself evident in her own increasing breaths, her rapid heartbeats. Had she really done such a stupid thing? Expose herself to this man, then expect he'd *not* want to ravish her?

Suddenly off her feet and cradled in the crook of two strong arms, Madeleine let out a squeak as she landed in the center of the bed. The velvet bed curtains tittered, setting the fringed border to a jerky dance. Armand's boots flew one way and then the other to land against the wall. His steel-pointed scabbard clanked against the carved armoire. Doublet and shirt were shed with the ease of much practice.

Madeleine scrambled to the head of the bed and clutched a pillow to her gut. A seductive devil with dark eyes and passion brewing in his raspy purrs stalked closer.

He'd lost all rational thought. Had completely forgotten about their agreement. Pray to the seven saints and Mother Mary, too! What to do?

Four

A staccato of raps outside the chamber door froze Armand and Madeleine upon the bed.

"Saint-Sylvestre?"

Recognizing the voice, Armand pressed a finger to his lips, beckoning Madeleine's silence as he slithered off the bed. She yanked the counterpane to her chin and wriggled down into the darkened depths of the canopy-shadowed tester. He dodged for his shirt and shoved his arms through the sleeves.

Hastening to the door, Armand slipped through without opening it any wider than his body. Captain Chance Lambert, a man who Armand hoped would become his leader should he prove himself worthy of a position in the musketeers, stood with a fist propped against the wall, his other hand working his main gauche in acrobatic circles between his fingers.

The man was also his brother-in-law, having married Armand's sister Mignonne a year ago. But it was obvious this was no family visit. The hour was late. Chance looked ready for action, showing no signs of having imbibed the party's liquor offering.

"Retiring early this fine evening?" the captain queried.

Remaining in front of the door, Armand crossed a foot over the other, then realized he wore no boots. Hell, he was disheveled. His shirt was untied and spilling over his breeches. "It's past midnight, I'm sure, Captain. Fouquet retired hours ago with a half dozen giggling wenches tucked beneath his arms. I presume he'll not be going anywhere until the morning. Even then, I'm sure he'll rise late."

"Pity the man who has to follow Fouquet from fête to fête. The financier is a social whore; he drinks in parties like a thirsty man fallen into a well. So you"—Chance tilted his head and made to look through the narrow crack between the door and the frame—"found your own bevy of beauties?"

"Well, I, er . . ."

He was officially off duty. But damn, if this situation didn't look bad for him.

Madame Saint-Sylvestre.

He still could not believe he'd let such a thing happen.

"I should never expect that Armand Saint-Sylvestre could give up women entirely," Chance said with a reassuring wink. "So is she saucy? Am I keeping you from anything?"

Anything? Armand swallowed. If the captain only knew.

"No, Captain. Well, I mean, yes." Armand felt a wide grin curl his lips. He propped a hand on the doorframe. "She is a saucy treat. But worry not, she is merely a diversion. I'll be up early in the morn to resume my duties. I've every intention of taking this assignment seriously if it will see me out of the foot troops and into the household guards. Can't have my own sister show me up as a musketeer, now, can I?"

"Indeed, Min had hoped you'd take to that challenge. But here now, I've come with new orders from Colbert. Tomorrow you ride to Vaux-le-Vicomte."

"Fouquet is leaving for his château?"

"No. According to the financier's secretary, Fouquet plans to remain in Paris for the next week. An excellent opportunity for you to search Vaux. The man has been planning a fête in the king's honor. Expenses are rumored to be remarkable. Colbert needs you to report your findings; excessive displays of wealth, exorbitant living conditions, and so on. Look for documents also. Colbert suspects Fouquet might be storing financial records at his home. They may be in code, so fetch anything that looks suspicious. You understand?"

"Certainly, I'll be off on the morrow."

"Good." Chance shoved his dagger into the leather scabbard at his waist. The man was soldier from toe to ear. Always ready for battle and never reluctant to draw first blood. "Oh, and Armand?"

Already pushing the door open. Armand paused halfway inside the bedchamber. Madeleine's scent seduced unmercifully. "Yes?"

"About this diversion you've got purring in your bed . . . A successful mission will provide your commission in the guards; don't forget what is most important."

Indeed. Had he already forgotten that he needed to earn his captain's trust? Had a little taste of woman rattled his good senses?

"Yes, well . . ." How could he expect to earn the captain's trust by keeping the truth from him now? And wouldn't Mignonne be upset to hear her brother was still lying to find his way in the world? "Actually . . ."

Chance's silence and raised brow were not helping Armand's dilemma. But if he could not be truthful with his own brother-in-law, then to whom could he speak the truth? Pride demanded he confess.

"Armand?"

Wasn't there honor in the truth? And wasn't honor the one thing he needed more than ever right now? "That's my wife lying in there on the bed." He parried a glance Lambert's way.

"Not by choice. It was sort of—it wasn't planned. Well—she was desperate."

Chance's eyes widened. He gripped his dagger again. "I see. And how long did you know this woman before you decided upon the irresistible urge to take vows?"

Armand counted on his fingers. "Half an hour, I'd say. I took pity on her situation. Her father is ill, you see. She's harmless, really. You are thinking I've slipped a wheel-pin, aren't you?"

"Your wife." Chance said the words as if to speak them would answer all the bizarre notions he might have. He slapped a firm hand on Armand's shoulder. "Nothing wrong with a night of debauchery. But marriage? A stunning confession coming from you, Saint-Sylvestre. She must be quite a charmer. Who is this woman who has snared one of France's most illustrious pretenders in her nets?"

"Madeleine . . . mm, well, I'm not sure of her maiden name. Well, Madame Saint-Sylvestre now. For the time, that is."

Ah hell, but didn't his confession reek of stupidity? This conversation was either completely destroying any chance of his being accepted into the guards, or else had convinced his brother-in-law that he was certifiably stupid. Neither of the two being particularly high on Armand's list of desired attributes. He could only imagine what Chance was thinking behind the cool reserve of his expression. Probably that his brother-in-law was a weak man for succumbing to such a ruse—definitely not guard material. Chance's smirk said it all.

"Believe me, this situation is only temporary. It will not impede my mission. In fact, perhaps I can use Madeleine as cover at Vaux. Two lovers vacationing at the fine château?"

"Nothing wrong with bringing a saucy wench along on vacation," Chance said, with a growing smile that flattened suddenly to a grimace. "But don't you think the fact that your brother tends the gardens at Vaux is reason enough to visit?"

Stating the obvious only made Armand feel all the more a

dupe. Of course, Alexandre had worked in the gardens of Vaux-le-Vicomte for the past year. It was high time he paid his brother a visit.

Thankfully, Chance rescued Armand from having to drum up an even lamer excuse for his stupidity. "I shall leave the master pretender to plot out his own cover. Colbert did choose you especially for your skills." Lambert shuffled his gloved hand through Armand's hair. "Just see that the wench doesn't interfere."

Chance excused himself, and Armand toyed with the curved gold grip on the chamber door. Is this how it had felt to be one of his victims? Unable to take control?

"Forgive me," he whispered heavenward, hoping that the God he had ignored for many years would bend an ear for just a moment. "Is this your way of teaching me remorse?"

But he did feel remorse for his past crimes. Though he'd never left a widow penniless; nor had he harmed any innocents. That they had fallen in love with him was beyond his control. It had all been an act, a necessity in order to gain their trust. A steel heart can no more sense emotion than a rock can ooze blood.

Now he found himself thrust into a bizarre scenario that absolutely reeked of his past crimes. Just what stake did Madeleine have in this plot?

Ah yes . . . Anything.

He would question her motives later. The moment demanded surrender to the mood. And a rather passionate mood they'd set, if Armand recalled correctly.

The bed curtain had been loosened from its braided restraint to shade one side of the bed. Most likely Madeleine had not wanted to be seen. As Armand pulled the heavy damask to the side he suddenly heard breathy purrs.

Snoring?

Just his luck.

Reaching over, Armand allowed his fingers to hover above

her nose as he considered an attempt to quelch the racket. She'd most likely wake, and they could resume their liaison. Copper tendrils twirled across the feather pillow. Her eyelids were smooth and laced with long, dark lashes. The urge to bend forward and kiss the candlelight-drenched skin was so strong. Oh, but this beauty, whose soft lips were parted, had the growl of a beast!

On second thought it would be best to allow sleeping beasts to lie. He traced the arc of one of her thick curls. Everywhere her delicious hair lay strewn across the pillow.

"What was the name of the she-creature that sported a head of snakes and would turn men to stone if they looked at her?" Armand whispered. "Ah yes, Medusa."

Armand hooked a coil of copper around his thumb. "I think I shall call you Medusa, my flame-haired beauty who would seduce me into your arms. You've already succeeded in turning me hard as stone."

The sun had barely risen above the line of silvery water that flashed from a distance in the Pond of the Swiss Guards. In sleep, Madeleine's body had contorted to cover much of the bed, so Armand had spent the night propped in an armed chair. The crick in his neck screamed with even the slightest movement, but he ignored it. Behind the drawn bed curtains she still slept, surprisingly, snoreless. He did not want to draw back the damask for a peek. No sense risking startling her awake when he had his own plans to tend to.

There had been a time when Armand had wished with every fiber of his being for a snoring woman in the mornings. Anything to aid his escapes. He'd been fortunate that his deceptions hadn't pushed him to dastardly deeds, such as murder. Hell, he'd never consider such evil.

Though lying and pretending to be something he was not was evil enough, he had always reasoned that it was done for the sake of his family. Antoine Saint-Sylvestre had died when Armand was fifteen. His brothers and sister were all younger, and with a mother that had passed upon his sister Mignonne's birth, Armand had become the master of the family literally by the draw of a sword. For Antoine, a former musketeer, had been taken down on a lonely high road by thieves, for nothing more than sport in claiming a musketeer's tunic.

Though he might have concentrated his efforts on revenge, at the time, there had been no choice offered Armand except to find a quick way to make money. Antoine's meager wages had laid bread and wine on the table, nothing more. Without a by-your-leave, Armand had been forced to take up the post as family caregiver to provide for three siblings. Alexandre had already developed an interest in botany and needed books to study. Adrian and Mignonne desperately needed clothing, for the hand-me-downs from two older siblings were threadbare and tight, and there was proper schooling to consider should Min ever hope to attract a worthy suitor.

A chance encounter while riding home from Paris one night found Armand riding up to a coach stopped roadside due to a broken wheel. A woman inside the carriage had shrieked at sight of his shadowed face and silent inquiry—and something had just clicked. Some inner need had twisted in his gut, pining for release, for satiation. Armand had drawn his pistol and ripped the jeweled necklace from her throat, leaving in a blaze of gunfire meant only to caution, never harm.

How circumstances had invited him into such a profession, he would always wonder. But the fact that he had continued to rob and eventually advance to the grand charade of pretending would forever mar his conscience, if not his honor.

Could he be trusted now? Of course Armand knew deep inside that he could. But trust must be earned, and he had no qualms with Captain Lambert requesting he prove himself before granting him a household commission.

Thinking of commissions . . . if he'd didn't saddle up soon, he'd lose any positive ground he'd gained with the captain.

Dressing quickly in shirt, doublet, and breeches, and securing his sword at his hip, Armand paused before the mirror to study the dash of the steel blade jutting from waist to calf. Five small emeralds were set in the bronze hilt. A prize gifted him by one of his conquests. One of the few regrets he had in the myriad list of victims he had tallied. She had fallen immediately in love with him. It had not been a selfish or vain love, as most of the women he'd happened upon were wont to feel. She had loved him blindly, opening her heart to his false advances. So naive, she had never a chance against his wiles.

He'd not the courage to go through with his plans to steal a quarter of her dead husband's fortune. He'd left as soon as he realized his folly. To this day Armand dared not utter her name for fear of invoking the weakness that had guided him out of her life in such a meek and shameful way.

But surely he owed the woman gratitude, for she had been the last of his victims, the one who had made him pause to think life through. The thrill of the crime had become just that. A thrill. His family no longer in need of support, Armand had turned away from pretending. And he owed it all to her—that woman whose name he dared not utter—but would remember every time he touched this sword.

If only to repay her—a gesture of retribution toward all his victims—he must better himself as a man.

A more tangible means of repayment was seen to every month with the anonymous delivery of half his wages to her estate. According to his own spy, Armand knew the woman's finances were in dire straits. And so he would do what little he could to assist her—though still it seemed a petty gesture to him.

Punching a fist in his opposite palm made him wince for the muscles that stretched in his back. This must be how the elderly felt, he thought, as each footstep pulled at his aching limbs.

Last night had been the first—and last—night he would not
sleep in a bed.

A spur chittered across the stone threshold, but as he turned
toward the bed he was reassured by the gold fringes sewn
around the canopy frame. Completely still.

Once in the outer hall, Armand closed the door carefully and
was able to release his held breath. A cool breeze moved a few
long hairs across his forehead, and the fresh tang of citrus
promised a tasty morning meal.

Pressing a hand to his aching back. Armand grimaced as he
eased his shoulders up and stretched out the kinks by rotating
his arms. He felt much worse than he thought the satisfaction
of *anything* should have made him feel.

"More retribution." he muttered with a glance toward
heaven. "I suppose I do deserve this."

Ah, but Madeleine had proven her lack of skill in this game
of deception she played. For if she had been a master, would
she not have spread her legs and invited him in?

Perhaps not. Armand rehashed his own experiences of insti-
gating himself into the lives of unsuspecting widows. The slow,
careful seductions always yielded the largest booty. Indeed,
perhaps Madeleine knew exactly what hand must be played,
and when. A formidable opponent, his Medusa.

Two doors down Armand found himself standing before an
open door. Inside, a valet poured aromatic tea for his master.
The wet barklike scent made Armand's stomach scream for
sustenance. The valet nodded, and without so much as a word
from Armand offered tea.

With relief, Armand eased inside and leaned against the wall.
"*Merci*. It seems I'm not up to par this morning. Slept in a
bad position. Tea would be most welcome—Papa!"

"And just what sort of position did you sleep in?" The old
man's hair-festooned face popped up from the pillow and
peeked around the embroidered bed curtains. He pulled the bed

sheets up to his chin, but the gray eyes glared like fire at Armand.

Could the morning get much worse? Armand felt the hunger in his gut begin to churn into a nauseating swirl.

"I actually slept—"

"I don't need to hear it!" the old man declared. He scanned the floor at his bedside and produced his cane. Wood clanged against wood as he slammed it across the night table. "Are you happy now? You've gotten exactly what you wanted."

"Monsieur, I . . ." Armand couldn't bring himself to casually sip the hot liquid. Another clang of the cane against the night table stiffened his shoulders and tightened the sore muscles in his back. The old devil had enough spunk for that of a man half his age.

"Papa, you mustn't be cruel."

Madeleine slipped from the opposite side of the bed, dressed in yesterday's plum gown, her hair elegantly coifed in a slick chignon, and her eyes shining brighter than the sun. Like a pair of exotically colored sweets, her eyes.

"Good morning, dear husband. I didn't wish to wake you, so I slipped out quietly. I wanted to check on Papa. Some of the king's guards have offered to transport him to Les Invalides. Isn't that generous of the king?"

Armand didn't know what to say. Hadn't he just left her behind? He could have sworn he'd heard a muffled snore at least once while dressing.

"Les Invalides," he said absently. "Yes. A fine military hospital. Though," Armand shouted over the repetitive clack of the cane, "it appears you're feeling much better this morning, Papa?"

"Huh? Oh." The old man clutched his chest. "You've riled me, boy." He hacked a dry cough, which he followed with a splendid series of choking heaves.

"You've upset him," the valet admonished. "The two of you should both leave."

"But I—"

The valet snatched the full cup of tea from Armand's groping fingers. So much for small mercies.

"Yes, we should leave him to rest." Madeleine touched Armand's shoulder and directed him toward the door.

"Treat her well ... *hack* ... Do not let her out of your sight!"

Madeleine closed the door with a careful click and let out a shoulder-lifting sigh. "He worries so about me."

"Not let you out of my sight?" So how was he going to work this one? "What does the old man want from me?"

"Just until he's well," Madeleine hastened to add, as Armand eased his way down a yew-lined stretch and across the black-and-white-checked marble courtyard toward the stables. Couldn't have a woman see he was weak. But damn, if he didn't want to let out a hearty groan.

"I promise I won't get in your way. I'll be like a ghost."

"Ghosts scare the hell out of me, Madame Medusa."

She scampered to his side as Armand found an easy pace that didn't tax his aching muscles. "What did you call me?"

"Medusa," he said. "And I've no intention of becoming tangled in your coils today, Madame. I'm to ride to Vaux."

"Vaux!"

His pace to the stables increased, his spurs clicking off the marble to stir up the dusty ground, but still the soft shuffle of Madeleine's silk slippers followed. She was huffing by the time he rounded the shadowed coolness of the sweet-smelling stables. Fresh straw, cleanly mucked gutters. He did like the aroma of wildness. It promised freedom and a certain calm. A sensation utterly missing in the busy city of Paris.

"But you can't leave me." Madeleine carefully plucked her way across the center gutter and tugged on Armand's sleeve. "I am your wife. You heard what Papa said, you're to keep me close. What about our agreement?"

A hefty inhale only drew in the heady perfume of Madeleine's creamy flesh. She wore amber as if a glove, a most enticing garment that enhanced its owner's attributes exquisitely.

Deep inside his gut Armand's hunger pangs pulsed. But it wasn't food this hunger required for satiation.

"Why are you going to Vaux?"

"I've a mission," he said, and turned away from her irresistible fragrance. A mount would need to be saddled up. The king only issued his prized black Friesians to musketeers and household troops, and unfortunately his own horse nursed an abscessed foot back home at the Saint-Sylvestre château under his brother Adrian's attentive care.

He scanned the shadow-cooled walls of the stable for a lackey.

"What sort of mission? I thought you were but a foot soldier?"

Like a frisky puppy seeking a thrown ball, Madeleine tailed Armand's every move as he paced from one side of the stables to the other. No sign of a stable hand. Extremely frustrating.

"What exactly is your work? Is it dangerous? Secretive?"

"Would you cease with the questions," he barked. "I need to extract evidence from—" No. He couldn't put it that way. Information must be carefully guarded. Damn, but he could not think straight with this woman teasing his senses!

"There is a situation at Vaux that demands my attention. And that is already more than you need to know. Now, if you'll be so kind as to step aside, I'll have to saddle up my own mount."

"Take me along." She laced her arms back over the iron gate that Armand wanted to open, using her whole body as a shield that repelled no more than a grand feast laid before a starving man. "Please. I've always wanted to see the gardens of Vaux. I've heard they're splendid in the summertime."

"Impossible."

"Armand," she pouted.

Madame Medusa assumed control of Reluctant Madeleine's

countenance. It was like watching a mask slip from out of the ether and onto her face. And this mask wielded pursed lips and big blue eyes in a way that made Armand want to kiss the pout away.

"What about *anything?*"

Had her voice sounded lower? Did the slightest purr trace her words?

Medusa teased a long finger along the delicious mounds barely concealed by her low-cut bodice. She twirled her fingertip lazily upon her right breast. A full, soft globe that offered delicious nights of suckling.

Armand swallowed, and turned away. This wasn't right. When had the roles of seducer and seducee become reversed? He'd always kept hold of his wits in the past, always holding the upper hand.

She followed him across the gutter to the tack room. "How shall I ever grant you anything if you leave me behind?"

The damned tack door was locked! "There is no room for you on a single-rider saddle."

"We'll take a carriage."

"I ride faster alone."

"The château will not disappear if you are delayed."

"I work alone!" he barked, and spun around to face the incessant chirps of challenge.

"I thought you claimed to be a rogue last night."

"Indeed, I had also been drinking."

"You seemed to possess all your faculties."

"And yet somehow, with a grasp on all my faculties, I still gained a wife. Explain that one to me."

"You're changing the subject."

The sudden intrusion of her lips against his set Armand off guard. How easily she was capable of a surprise attack. And he always fell for it!

Sandwiching her body against the stable gate with his own body, Armand abandoned his less-than-stalwart resolve and pushed his hands up through her Medusa curls. He kissed her deep and fisted greedy handfuls of her hair over and over again. In an instant, his level of desire rocketed to the plateau he'd reached last night. The taste of her tongue told him she'd sipped chocolate this morning. The urgency of her moans signaled she'd been truthful in her agreement to see to the end her promise of anything.

He could lift her skirts right here. There was not a lackey in sight.

"Tonight," she gasped between kisses. "If you don't take me along, it'll never happen."

"It can happen right now," he growled.

"In need of a mount—er, excuse me, Monsieur."

Madeleine ripped away from the kiss at the lackey's interruption. Where the hell had he come from? Armand thought with mouth open wide and tongue still mourning the loss of Madeleine's delicious flavor.

"Actually, we'll be needing a coach," Madeleine instructed the blushing young man. In the next instant she cooed a giggle and tossed Armand a valiant wink.

Armand pressed his forehead to a supporting beam. Had he just missed something? When had the victory been claimed?

"Monsieur, are you ill?"

A punch to the thick wood beam gave Armand reason enough to rip out a vicious growl. The lackey thought it the pain of his stupid action; Armand knew it was the pain of having given Madeleine the victory once again, when he knew he could easily ride without her.

But somehow this defeat had a sweet edge to it. Yes. He would be the victor. But not until he'd gotten his just reward for putting up with Madame Medusa's ploy.

The view from over the tip of his red-damask shoe was a lush one at that. Amidst a myriad of workers raising columns and marble statues, and plasterers measuring walls, and gilders eyeing the ornate cornices—for the hunting lodge was, as of late, in a constant state of refurbishment—lay an elegant beauty that drew the eye away from the disaster of loose-lying stones and bricks and piping.

The Grande alley provided a view to the blushed azure horizon, underlined by frothy hedges of emerald treetops. Fully matured trees had been carted from across the ocean, it was rumored, so that King Louis would not have to endure the wait of a forest.

Of course, the hunting lodge-cum-palace paled in comparison to Vaux. The king had yet to discover the talents of his secret weapons, Le Nôtre, Le Brun, and Le Vau, gardener, painter, and architect, respectively. Ah, but what the king did not have was truly a boon to his own personal collection.

Nicholas Fouquet's view was suddenly spoiled by the interference of a gawky scatter of limbs and flailing coattails and powdered hair. And everywhere, wild magenta ribbons. Paul de Pellison wandered toward Fouquet's waiting carriage.

"I've been waiting something like ten minutes," Fouquet spit out, as his secretary stepped up into the carriage, forcing the financier to have to pull his feet down from their perch upon the door. "What the hell are you so out of breath for? And why"—he mined for the lace handkerchief stuffed up his sleeve and pressed it to his nose—"do you smell like a dead beast?"

"It is from the stables." De Pellison huffed as he studied the bottom of his shoes, found the reason for the odor, and removed them ever so carefully, so as not to actually touch the offending substance. "Look at this disaster. They are a complete loss. This fabric alone cast me two hundred pistoles."

"Toss them out. Quickly," Fouquet demanded through the lace kerchief. "What were you doing in the stables? That's quite out of your habitat."

"Following your spy." De Pellison fluffed at the looped ribbons bordering the hem of his petticoat breeches.

"She has succeeded'?"

"Beyond your expectations."

"Well done," Fouquet said. "We've got Saint-Sylvestre right where we want him."

"Tupping the redheaded wench?"

"The means to an end. Once the man falls in love—or even lust—it won't be difficult to wrench his secrets from him. Then I shall finally learn who is really spying on me. You're oozing."

Paul touched his cheek where Fouquet pointed. The heavy theatrical makeup used to give him a livid countenance slugged down his face. "This is worse than cold mash," he grumbled.

De Pellison brushed a hand across his face, noted the thick hair above his eyes, and jerked the eyebrows from his skin. "Ouch! Damned paste pulls out my own hair. Why did *I* have to play the old man?"

"You lend to the part well. Besides, you've a rather undistinguished visage; it takes well to disguise. You were not seen by Saint-Sylvestre?"

"No, save as Papa."

Fouquet replaced his feet upon the carriage door and tapped a fingernail against his lower front tooth. He had to learn why the man pursued him. Why else would a pretender be following him about? Did he have plans to rob him blind? Or something more sinister?

How things had so nicely slipped into order was fortune indeed, Fouquet mused now. 'Twas opportune he had learned of Madeleine de Pellison during one of his visits to his niece, Valérie Déscouvertes's sickbed. The woman was once an actress, Valérie had admiringly said of the woman she'd chosen to watch after her son. She is beautiful and smart and kind and had inherited a large sum from her husband's estate.

That was when the connection to his secretary had tapped Fouquet's brain. Paul made no secret of his intentions to prove his sister-in-law ineligible in order to gain his brother's fortune. Though he'd yet to hit on anything that would prove his claims, poor, stupid man that de Pellison was.

Ah, but this pawn Fouquet had chosen to spy on his spy . . .

It would take money to support a child. Madeleine had money. As long as she did exactly what he asked and reported Saint-Sylvestre's every move to him. For he was not beyond giving de Pellison the reason he needed.

"I still don't understand why we had to use that bitch to follow the man around. The whole plot is just so damned complicated. Why not just kill the man and have done with it?"

"And never discover for whom he works?"

Then there was the delicious notion that it would be an incredible coup to have a former highwayman on his side. Would put some of the more indelicate aspects of Fouquet's profession into the hands of a more capable minion. Ah, there was just so much a man could do with a criminal like Armand Saint-Sylvestre! The very thought made the saliva pool in Fouquet's mouth.

"Still, it is a twisted scenario this whole marriage thing," de Pellison said, now occupied with plucking the paste from his eyebrows.

"It keeps our spy close to the other spy. Besides, I rather enjoy toying with other people's lives."

"This I know. But the last person I wish to associate myself with is my former sister-in-law. The wench inherited a fortune upon my brother's death, a fortune that should have been mine," de Pellison sniffed.

"You know Pierre's heart had been troubling him since birth. The slightest loud noise could set him off. I'm surprised the faintheart made it as far as his wedding night. I shouldn't be surprised that the act of lovemaking took his final breath."

"Must we discuss the details? The woman is a murderess."

"As unfortunate as the fact is, the woman did not murder

your brother, unless you consider a beautiful face and spread legs a murder weapon.''

No, Fouquet did not believe Madeleine capable of murder. He suspected the vows were not legal for reasons Madeleine was keeping a tight lip about. And the very fact that she had agreed to do his bidding proved to Fouquet that the woman had something to hide regarding her wedding night. And he was prepared to play her bluff.

''Pierre's estate should have been remitted to me upon his death.'' Paul clamped his arms across his chest and stabbed the air with his sharp-tipped nose. Smeared makeup and a dangling eyebrow made him more ridiculous than his usual attire always did.

''And it shall be yours, in time.''

''In time, yes, yes. So you say. But when?''

''Saint-Sylvestre has taken the bait. Now we shall let him eat it.''

''As they are traveling to Vaux?''

''What?''

''I just overheard a curious conversation between the two of them. Saint-Sylvestre is on to Vaux—''

''Vaux? My—''

''Yes.'' De Pellison smoothed a wrinkle from his voluminous breeches and fussed with a strand of thread, stalling, Fouquet knew, for effect. The thick-skulled man did thrive on his dramatic moments.

''Out with it then. How do you know he is going to Vaux? And whatever for?''

''I heard him tell her straight he was going to Vaux and hadn't plans to take her along. But within a moment's time she'd attached herself to him like the worst kind of brothel whore and kissed him silly, and now he's mooing at her ankles, preparing a carriage for their joint departure.''

''Really? Well, at least we know our spy is gifted. Hmm . . .'' Fouquet squinted against the sun to get a better view of the goings on outside the stable doors. Saint-Sylvestre was nowhere in sight, nor was his flame-haired spy. "This is most vexing. What reason would the man have to travel to my home?"

"Perhaps they have joined forces. The thief and a murderess," de Pellison spit.

"Unfortunate." Fouquet twisted the tip of his narrow mustache between two fingers as he pondered his schedule for the next week. He had much to do in Paris before returning to Vaux to see to the final party preparations.

Why, all of a sudden, did Saint-Sylvester find his home of interest? Damn it, anyway, for whom did he work?

Five

Sure as snow falls in the winter, the bone-thin ragged street elf stood waiting outside the west entrance to Nôtre Dame. Leaving Madeleine in the carriage with the excuse that he could not leave Paris without saying a prayer for his grandmother, Armand skirted the smudge-faced boy and entered the cool shadows of the grand cathedral. "Most punctual," Armand said as he lifted his purse and checked its jingling contents. Not as much as he'd like to be in there, but he was working on that. "An extra sou for you this time."

He handed the boy his purse, then laid three sous in his grimy palm. The boy could barely contain his joy; his legs quivered as he studied the additional sou, turning it over and over. Armand had hired the youngster months ago after watching him one afternoon near the public well just down the street from his apartment. The urchin had been following the winding path of a caterpillar down the side of a stucco building, his wide brown eyes fascinated. Ever so carefully he'd prodded the fuzzy beast onto his palm for a closer view.

Just like Alexandre, Armand had thought of the boy. Curious and eager to learn. He sensed he could trust the boy with a mission that Armand could not handle himself. Every month, after receiving his wages, he earmarked half, and sent it to its destination in the hands of the youth.

That he wanted the purse to contain a thousand times more than what it held would never cease to punish Armand's conscience. But he would do what he could, until he could provide better.

"Why did we come inside today, Monsieur?" the boy asked. "Won't the lady you send this money to be jealous of the red-haired pretty in the carriage?"

"You know too much for your own good," Armand said with a tousle of the boy's grimy locks. "Be gone with you now. And swiftly, so the pickpockets and street rabble won't have a chance to clamp on to you."

"Thank you, Monsieur!" the boy yelled out as he skittered toward the front stairs of the cathedral and dashed into the blinding daylight.

The spire of Nôtre Dame passed on her left and receded into the background of rooftops, chimney smoke, and powderpuff clouds as the carriage ambled toward the Porte St. Michel.

Armand's devotion to his family touched Madeleine. A prayer for his grandmother? How thoughtful. Too thoughtful for a spy.

Oh, what was she thinking? There was certainly nothing wrong with being concerned for family. Spy or otherwise.

The ill effects of this morning's scene with Papa behind her, Madeleine felt confident the days to come could only improve. She had successfully insinuated herself into this blackguard's life. Fouquet only wished to know the man's actions; it shouldn't be so difficult to observe and report back.

Armand must love her before he could trust her enough to spill his secrets.

While she wasn't entirely sure what made one person fall in love with another, the notion that it either happened immediately or else took a very long time, like months, made her decide she must work for the immediate outcome. She wasn't sure Valérie had months. She might have guardianship of Stephan very soon.

But Armand was still reeling from last night's deception, and most certainly he was at great odds at finding himself a husband after nothing more than a kiss and a few minutes of heavy breathing. So Madeleine would pull back, play a bit more subtle, until she sensed he was comfortable around her.

Padded leather, smelling of lemon oil, decorated the interior of the carriage. The air breezing through the windows swirled single ticklish strands of Madeleine's hair across her chin.

She glanced unobtrusively across the small coach. Armand had slept in the chair near the bed all night. Thank the heavens her snoring act had worked! For as much as she found she desired this man, it would have been difficult to go through with *anything* last night. She wasn't yet comfortable around this alluring man. Though desire was quickly overcoming her wariness.

The surface of Armand's sword hilt caught the sun, and Madeleine's interest grew. "That's an interesting sword. Is it bronze?"

"Mm," he offered with a disinterested shrug. "A gift."

"From a lady friend?"

He cocked an eye open, speared her, and closed it again. No comment, not even a mumble.

So it *was* from a woman. And most likely stolen, Madeleine presumed. How audacious of the man to display his booty so brazenly.

"Last night you said you were a rogue. A man without ties

or money. How can a mere foot soldier possibly be on a mission? To Vaux? Tell me please what you do.''

"If you must know, I've a mission assigned by one of the king's ministers," he offered with a yawn, then tucked his hands under his arms and tilted his head forward, gifting Madeleine with the top of his black-plumed hat.

"I'm impressed. In the period of an evening you've gone from rogue to trusted, er . . . what exactly is your position?''

"It is of no matter to you, Madame." He looked up. The wide band of white lace circling his neck bent upward, which he irritatingly flicked away. "In fact the only thing of great importance on your schedule is to please your husband. You haven't forgotten our bargain?''

No, she had not. And she would not. If there were to be any remuneration for her part in this deception, she certainly hoped it would involve touches and kisses, and yes, even the consummation of the passions of which she had only dreamed.

"How long shall we stay at Vaux? I've only a few toiletries and the dress on my back.''

Armand tilted his hat brim up and studied her with sleepy regard. But beneath the heavy lids shone wide observant eyes. "Madame, it was you that pined desperation to accompany me on this trip. You should have thought of your own needs before we departed.''

"I had less than an hour to prepare.''

"Shall I drop you at the city gates and journey on without you?''

"No. No, I'll just have to make do. I wouldn't want to seem a bother. You've been kind enough as it is.''

Yes, by all means be agreeable, she coached inwardly. *Remain attached to the man at all costs so you don't miss a single move. That was the reason for the marriage in the first place.*

"Sit back. You've only to enjoy lounging about and traipsing through the gardens. I should think it a welcome respite from hovering over your father's sickbed. What more could a woman ask?''

Absolutely nothing. It would be a dream to have the leisure Armand spoke of. To loll about in the gardens, losing her cares upon a soft breeze. Never to have to worry that any person should wish to bring her world to a crumbling halt.

But she hadn't time to relax. She had a mission also.

"Now, we've already agreed that you shall serve me as a wife for the entire time that I must be forced to remain in this ridiculous excuse of a marriage. So if you abhor the idea of idling at Vaux, than you'd best pray Papa makes a miraculous recovery so you may be released from the marriage.''

"Hmmph.''

Armand rested the side of his head against two fingers, studying her for the longest time. "Tell me, there is a deeper reason for trapping me in this marriage, isn't there? I saw such desperation in your eyes last night. Beyond that of a woman concerned over her sick father.''

"I don't know what you mean. Isn't wishing for my father's dying request to be granted reason enough? And you've already discerned my lack of dowry.''

He shrugged and looked out the window. When he frowned, faint creases furrowed on his forehead.

"Just rather strange . . .'' he said on an absent tone. "Marrying as if it were but a party game. I've always thought marriage a sacred trust.''

"It is, and will be. After father has passed and this marriage is dissolved I shall marry for love,'' Madeleine said decidedly. "If and when it ever comes.''

He let out a smirking chuckle. "I see you're a dreamer as well as a schemer.''

"What is wrong with wishing for love?''

"Hmm?'' Armand pressed a thumb to his lower lip, analyzing her expectant gaze. "Oh. Love,'' he drew out the word in a mocking tone. "Love is a grandiose dream clutched to the hearts of many a young maiden. It is but a word, Madeleine. Exalted in prose and flowered in poetry. Too often it is muddied and twisted by the hands of any and all who would believe it possesses some magical power over their lives."

"Have you never had love?"

"Never wanted it," he answered quickly. Too quickly.

"What about giving it? I'm sure a man of your charm and allure has had many a woman fall in love with him."

"Never." Another quick answer.

But Madeleine suspected otherwise. "At least not that you are aware of."

"You imply something of which you've no knowledge, nor should you have knowledge."

"Ah, so you *have* left a lovesick woman or two in your wake?"

Arrow-true eyes worked upon her face. Madeleine retained her indifferent pose. But inside she quaked at the knowledge that she had struck a nerve. He might believe he has no desire for love, but what human did not wish a kind word, a caring touch?

Of course, his past crimes involved toying with innocent women's affections. Perhaps he'd twisted the core of the emotion so thoroughly he did not know true love anymore. Might not recognize it if it bit him on the nose?

Or kissed him on those enticing lips.

"My past is of no concern to you. As for love, I'm sure you'll get your wish someday. As soon as you can distance yourself from the deceit that seasons your life. Your father, as twisted as his heart may be, was only concerned for your well-being in his trickery. Though his logic regarding plucking a stranger out from a crowd does stun me. Tell me, are there no relatives that might provide for your dowry? Family? Perhaps a distant cousin that might take you in until love comes to you?"

Cousin? Not one that was well enough, or financially secure. She shrugged. "I've only my mother and Papa."

"Mother? And where is she? I had thought it was just you and your father?"

Oops. Cecile had not been a part of the script she and Fouquet had plotted. Madeleine gripped her faltering resolve and improvised. "She's at the—well, she is . . . indisposed at the moment."

More truthfully, off to Venice with her latest lover. The flavor of the month changed so frequently Madeleine had lost count of exactly how many lovers her mother had over the years. "You see, she and my father, well they do not speak. Never."

That was truth enough. Why, Madeleine couldn't even be sure who her real father was. The last time she'd laid eyes on him she'd been in infant skirts. "I chance to say they haven't had words with one another."

"Ever?"

"Well . . . of course." She shifted her gaze from his, out the window where tall reeds of heather brushed the sky with fuchsia paint, then back to her lap. "Cecile, my mother, used to attend to the Duchess le Reaux, until . . . well . . . she and my father do not live with one another. She resides in Venice now, I believe."

"You believe?"

Madeleine nodded, hoping he'd accept that. To delve too deeply into her relationship with her mother would only spoil her concentration and show her for the desperate, lonely woman she had become.

"That's not good. A woman should never be left alone without some family by her side and the finances to keep her secure."

Valiant words coming from a man who had just refused to involve himself in any conversation dealing with emotion.

"I shall have family someday."

How his sudden regard, eagle-eyed and fierce, always set Madeleine off guard! "You say the word as if it were an object, not a gathering of caring individuals."

"No, it's not an object." She tilted her head, a thoughtful dream of the perfect way of things coming to mind.

"I imagine family is not necessarily a thing, or a place, or even a person. It is a feeling. A well-being. A deep, heartfelt trust and love. Family should be the one place where I can leave my heart without fear of it being broken."

"You speak as though it is something you have never had."

"Perhaps." Her hopeful gaze followed the flight of a crow skimming the distant ribbon of treetops.

"So tell me how a woman, obviously raised at court, comes to find herself dowerless?"

"Oh? Oh."

Madeleine would never lack for finances thanks to her departed husband's estate. As long as Paul de Pellison did not discover her secret regarding the wedding night, that estate could never be challenged. She knew Fouquet had just been guessing that she had something to hide. But if he challenged that guess, her life would be shattered.

So how would she explain this lack of dower that Armand had assumed—much out of the script, but believable enough at the time that she had agreed to it?

"Well, Papa . . . he um . . . gambled it away." Believable enough! "I believe his sickness is a direct result of years spent gambling and drinking. Vice does take its toll. But what of *your* family?"

Yes, it was his turn. This digging into her family history would only throw her out of character. "You've mentioned a sister and a brother thus far. What of your parents?"

"My parents have long since died." Armand removed his hat and toyed with the feather, easing the frothy plume through his curled forefingers. "My father was a musketeer." He uttered the title in an awe-filled tone.

"Really? How honorable." So why had Armand veered so far from the path? "And you've no desire to carry on a family tradition?"

"Of course I do. Just isn't as easy as marching up to the king and demanding a commission."

"I'm sure. You said yourself you are a rogue."

He raised a brow at that remark. Knowledge of his past or not, something about the word *rogue* fit Armand Saint-Sylvestre as if a personalized glove. But another part of the word, a darker, more sinister part slid over him like rain on freshly tanned hide. And that fact vexed Madeleine to no end. It was his charm. She was falling victim to his charm.

Not an entirely undesirable way to fall, either.

He stretched his legs out sideways until his spurs clicked against the opposite door and draped his arm against the veneer wall both sat near. "I am a rogue shackled by the unexpected responsibility of a wife."

"I see no shackles on your wrists."

"You would allow me to walk away from our bargain?"

"You would want to? After you were practically drooling over the prospect of bedding me?" She looked away. This brazen act was new to her. But it came with such ease it shocked her.

That she had been denied pleasure too long would surely be her downfall.

"Ah yes, the slow seduction," he said, perusing her expression with glittering interest. "I'm having difficulty figuring you out, Madeleine. Perhaps you can assist me?"

"Whatever do you mean?"

"You promise to end this marriage. You act as though it means nothing to you beyond pleasing your father, and yet . . . a part of you really wants this."

"No."

"Oh yes." With a bend of his knees, Armand lunged forward and seated himself at her side. Madeleine scooted away, but the wall of the carriage stopped her. The light pressure of his finger, skimming beneath her chin, worked an incredible spell that made her inhibitions melt, her shoulders fall, and her head settle back against the padded wall behind her.

"You wanted my kisses last night," he whispered. He skimmed his finger over her lips, a sculptor mapping the dimensions of his marble statue. "Can you say you did not?"

"I—I did. I do," she whispered. "I do like your kisses. But that doesn't mean—"

Protest ceased with a deep, gut-tingling kiss. They slipped into a perfect embrace of lips and heavy breaths and searching fingers. Armand reached round and drew his fingertips along the center of Madeleine's spine, compelling her body to arch forward against his as he caressed the small of her back. His unbound hair curled across her cheeks and tickled her eyelids. Male lust smelled exotic and forbidden.

She wanted this kiss . . . "Forever," Madeleine whispered into Armand's mouth. "Kiss me forever. Just like this."

He sucked her lower lip and nibbled languorously. "Like this?"

"That's . . . oh . . . marvelous."

"How about this?" He kissed her quickly; Madeleine's lips parted, then closed; then he traced the seam of her mouth with the point of his tongue. "Open," he whispered. He softened his strokes and slipped his tongue up behind her upper lip, marking a path that ignited her every nerve ending, from her prickling hairline down to her curling toes.

"Admit it," he said, pulling back to study her. "You want me as much as I want you."

Of course she did. But he was cheating! How could she possibly say no when his fingers skimmed over her breasts, and his lips glistened with the promise of more masterful kisses? If she surrendered, gave in at this very moment, could they have more than simple pleasures of the flesh?

Something held Madeleine back from completely surrendering her body to its desires. Some tiny niggling at the base of her brain demanded she not lay herself before this man like a tavern whore whose knees had not brushed against one another since she'd starting serving ale.

Don't fall victim to his charms.

She must remain in character. Abandon her real feelings and desires, and allow the actress to thrive.

"I want you, Madeleine." Heavy exhales accompanied his words. As she continued to struggle with right and doing-what-must-be-done, Armand trailed his tongue down her chin and nuzzled his nose against the curve of her neck. "Tell me you want me."

The tracing of his tongue up and down and in tiny circles on her neck did things to Madeleine. Strange things. Exciting things. Wild things!

Her knees weakened, and Armand hooked a hand beneath her thigh. The whisper of his fingers gripping her silk skirts sounded sinful, divine. She arched her bosom toward his chest and tilted her head back to better expose the sensitive flesh on her neck to his devastating tongue. Gasps and moans slipped unbidden from her mouth. An erotic hum began in her loins. The scent of passion, of want, filled her nostrils.

She fleetingly realized her motions had settled the two of them in a horizontal position. Armand knelt upon the carriage floor, while her head was jammed against the padded wall. She slunk down and raked her fingers through the thick crop of dark curls skimming her breasts. "Yes, I want you," she panted. "But not like this. Not in this cramped space—oh, Armand."

He'd not even untied the bows securing her bodice, yet her movements had eased her nipple close to the lace trim of her chemise. Armand's tongue darted in and out of her bodice, spearing the aching pebble of flesh. He did not try to work the lace lower, nor to untie the ribbons.

Foolish man.

Madeleine clutched the top ribbon and pulled it straight. A

heavy exhale brought her nipple up into Armand's mouth, an undulating, hot portal of passion. What this man could do to her with just his mouth! It was incredible. Stunning. She wanted it never to stop. If this was the beginning of what could only promise to become more intense, she decided resistance would be a ridiculous thing.

She was a married woman. There was nothing to stop her from having the passion she desired. This man might very well fall in love when offered the one thing he wanted.

The snap of leather against the outer wall of the carriage brought Armand up from his exquisite torture. The lace of his sleeve cuff brushed her nipple, stirring a moan up from her loins. Madeleine clung to him as he scanned out the window.

"We've arrived," he announced with a sly smirk. "We're rolling down a long alley of hedgerows that must lead up to the gardens." On a heavy sigh he said, "I suppose you are right about this cramped carriage. It does leave a bit to be desired. Shall we resume our exploration of *anything* later, Madame Saint-Sylvestre?"

Madeleine placed his palm over her breast. "As long as you don't forget where you left off."

He dipped his head and parted his fingers to allow her nipple to slip through them. Two quick lashes of his tongue threatened to make Madeleine command the driver to turn back for Paris—and get lost on the way.

"I've marked my spot," he said. "Now there's no possible way of forgetting."

As they gained the main grounds, the openmouthed expression on Madeleine's face told Armand all he needed to know of Vaux's rumored extravagance.

Armand had come to learn from Colbert that the Superintendent of Finances couldn't possibly have the income to afford such luxury. Of course, Jean-Baptiste Colbert was known to bother over nothing. His nickname around court was the North Wind, on account of his stingy ways and usual frown. But court intrigue did not matter to Armand. All that did was that he had been given a chance to prove himself and to begin anew.

Finally, his years of pretending could be put to more honest intentions. Skills such as wearing a facade of indifference, stealth, and discretion were important weapons in his arsenal. Even his seduction skills had come into play.

Armand glanced to Madeleine. Recalling the feel of her nipple slipping across his tongue made his mouth water. She would be as easy as all the rest to seduce into bed. Already he believed she might have stepped quite a few levels down from her original stand against going slow.

Oh, he would go slow. The proper pacing would have Madeleine begging for him to take her before Papa could spring out of his sickbed. Like tonight. Wasn't that slow enough?

Besides, he wasn't about to let her off without payment of *anything*. He had agreed to help her. She would repay in kind.

High walls of blue-green yew queued past the carriage window. The scent of clean summer air reminded Armand of the Saint-Sylvestre château that sat twenty leagues south of Paris. Adrian remained, tending the few horses the family owned, and keeping the grounds. The youngest brother had no great desires, beyond a full belly and the occasional tavern wench— aspirations to see any man through life without worry or unnecessary financial need. Armand smiled.

Madeleine drew her head inside from the window and sighed. "It's very grand."

"Perhaps a bit too grand."

"Why do you say that?"

"No reason." That he could tell her.

Double formal gardens stretched in two straight lines before the château. Rust-hued stone served as background for knee-high yews coaxed into curving flourishes, while the straight carriage aisles were a pale bleached stone. To his right, fat lily pads dotted a wide pond. Three marble steps down from there stretched another vast garden. Not many flowers in the extravagant design of shrubbery and stone, but here and there a flash of red caught Armand's eye.

A few people dotted the grounds, some wielded smoked glass set in ornate metal frames to protect their eyes from the sun. Telescopes were set up to view the horizon, while others, women, strolled beneath lace-edged parasols, their wide skirts dusting the grasses. Armand squinted to make out the faces of each and every one. He had to be here somewhere. . . .

What Madeleine had said earlier about family. *It is a place to leave my heart.*

Even an armored heart?

"Ah!" A familiar face ripped Armand from deeper thoughts. "There's Alexandre. Stop just ahead," Armand shouted to the driver. "We shall say hello to my brother and then we can walk up to the château."

"Your brother? He works at Vaux?"

"Yes, he's an assistant to the head gardener, Le Nôtre. He and his wife and their twin daughters have lived here for a year now. I was hoping he'd be around; it's been months since I've seen him."

"Than I can't wait to meet him myself. Is it just the three of you then, two brothers and one sister?"

"Adrian lives at home still. The four of us, it is. But I don't think it'll be necessary to tell my brother we are married."

"Oh?" Her smile slipped from those tasty ruby lips. But the sparkle in her eyes remained. "No, I imagine it won't be necessary." A formidable opponent, indeed. "So what are we then?"

Armand reached and adjusted the bow she'd retied, drawing his thumb across her breast as he retreated. "Lovers, of course. Are you up for the challenge?"

She straightened her shoulders and drew herself regally upright. "Are you?" she teasingly challenged.

How Armand admired Madeleine's spirit. And that flushed alabaster skin.

The carriage wobbled to a halt, but Armand remained as Madeleine pushed the door open. He helped her down and stepped onto the crushed stones in a muffled clatter of rock. "You, my lady, haven't a clue as to whom you are dealing with."

"Tell me . . ." Madeleine narrowed her gaze on him and pursed her kiss-plumped lips. "Whom *am* I dealing with?"

Taken off guard, Armand stumbled for a witty return, but didn't imagine "the Gentleman Thief, a man who'd once seduced women for a living" would sit too well with his wife.

On the other hand, she did seem just audacious enough to rather enjoy that bit of information.

"You shall discover soon enough." Even as he muttered the words, he couldn't help consider whom *he* was dealing with. With whom *was* he dealing?

She tugged on his hand, an entreaty to step closer to her side. "Don't you trust me?"

"Trust?" Armand narrowed his gaze on her innocent query. "Madame, I make it a point to trust no one. You see already the predicament a moment of relaxed guard has placed me in. Now, shall we?"

He directed her toward the center of the left garden, where his brother had spied them, and now walked toward the carriage, arms swinging briskly and flowing mass of dark hair flagging out behind his shoulders.

"Of course. But first." She gripped his shoulders and planted a kiss on Armand's lips. Too quick. Not potent enough. But . . . promising.

"What was that for?"

"We *are* playing lovers."

"But Madame, you are grossly mistaken." He swept her into his arms and pressed a hard kiss to her semi-open mouth. Focused only on marking her with the heavy desire that had burned itself into his bones, Armand did not release her until he was sure the target had been hit. "There."

She wobbled backward, touching her lips with a gloved finger.

"That, Madame Medusa, is how lovers should kiss."

Pleased, Armand hooked an arm around his stunned pupil's waist and prepared to begin phase one of his mission. Lying to his brother.

Six

Alexandre Saint-Sylvestre much resembled his brother in complexion and dark hair, but beyond that, there was quite a difference between the cavalier spy Madeleine had married and the wisp of a gardener who now kissed her cheek in welcome.

Alexandre resembled a lithe, flowing willow to Armand's proud oak. Fingertips stained green fiddled with his free-flowing elbow-length hair in an attempt to dislodge it from his eyelashes. Finally, he gave up with a shrug.

Huffing up behind Alexandre appeared a woman whom he introduced as his wife, Sophie. Red velvet skirts *swooshed* across the pebbled walk as she hooked an arm in her husband's and nodded curtly at introductions. No gesture to establish a friendly touch, not even with her gray eyes. With a bounce of her tightly coiled blond curls, Sophie assessed Madeleine's uncomfortable composure with a triumphant jerk of her head.

Neither of the two paid much attention to the toddlers crawling about the pebbles. Not quite two years old, Madeleine estimated given their pudgy faces and awkward wobbles. It was a good thing a maid attended the children, as she noticed one of the girls shove a handful of stones into her mouth.

"What brings you to Vaux, Armand?" Sophie cooed, granting him all her attention, Madeleine noticed. And the woman seemed quite pleased that Madeleine did notice. "It has been far too long."

"Yes, and why should he need an excuse?" Alexandre spoke over his wife's pouting declaration. "Such a lovely traveling partner." Madeleine did not miss the hopeful note in Alexandre's voice. He seemed genuinely delighted to meet her, as opposed to his wife's staunch refusal even to acknowledge her. "Come to spend a few days in the luxurious château? Or are you arriving early for the fête?"

"No, no, I don't attend parties. Anymore," Armand said.

Madeleine caught the annoyance in his statement of *anymore.* As if he'd been denied something he'd once lavished upon himself. Of course he had to have attended all number of parties when he'd been stealing from innocent people.

"I've heard much of Vaux. I thought to admire its grandness myself, and at the same time check up on my brother's work. It is stunning, Alexandre, what you can do with shrubs and stones. You've so much talent it is truly blinding."

Alexandre accepted his brother's compliment with a bow and a slight rosing of his cheeks. "Le Nôtre must be considered master of creation here at Vaux. I have learned much from the man in so short a time."

"You seem quite happy."

Madeleine noticed Sophie roll her eyes toward the clouds and shove a fist against her hip. Alexandre reached for his wife's hand and jerked it down between the two of them. He offered a congenial smirk to Madeleine. "She finds it difficult to be away from Paris."

"Must you speak for me as if I hadn't a voice?" Sophie wrenched her hand from her husband's clutch. Each curt motion set the froth of curls mushrooming each ear to a titter. "So

Armand, what has it been, a mere two weeks since we've last seen you in Paris? There was no mention of Madeleine then.''

"It's been longer than that," Alexandre threw in his brother's defense. "More than a month, perhaps even two. Give the man credit, Sophie, I think it great fortune my brother has taken the time to bring a woman into his life. And such a lovely one at that.''

"You've said as much already," Sophie snapped.

"How long have the two of you been together?"

"Er—"

"Not long," Madeleine broke in over Armand's reply. "Actually, we've only just met, but when your brother and I started talking about Vaux and he expressed an interest, I simply begged to accompany him. I've been in desperate need of a holiday in the country. The Paris air is simply horrid during the hot summer months. And the stench. I do believe the city has been quite lax in gutter control lately. A woman cannot even go to market without dirtying her skirts and bringing the foul odor home in her hem.''

"You'll find that Vaux is no different." Sophie jerked her head toward the grand gray-brick facade of the château. "Since the party arrangements have begun, the dust and shouting never cease. Beware your step, for horses are paraded about in efforts to raze a tree here and erect a stage there. I haven't slept for weeks, for the tremor of hooves echoes in my head even after the sun has fallen.''

"I'll have to remember that," Madeleine said with a glance to Armand.

He ignored her and scanned the grounds, where indeed Madeleine did notice a team of horse and carts hauling what looked like lengths of wood around behind the château.

Had Armand's sudden trip here something to do with the fête Fouquet was preparing for the king? If he was truly spying on Fouquet, wouldn't he need to stay close to the man? Or did he have a more sinister plan that might involve theft, perhaps even pretending?

"Just what is all the upset?" Armand asked his brother. "You say there's a party?"

"Fouquet has been planning this affair for months. I'm surprised you haven't caught wind of it in Paris. He's addicted to building and remodeling and expanding the gardens. He cannot walk down an aisle of hedges without plucking a stray leaf here and there, or rearranging a mussed pile of stones that missed raking. The man is a perfectionist."

"I can't imagine the expense."

But he could imagine spending the money, Madeleine thought as she threaded an arm through Armand's. But to think now, if he had spent years stealing, what *had* become of his riches? He'd made her to believe he was quite poor, a mere foot soldier. Though he dressed beyond the means of such low rank. Hmm . . . Had he lived such a life of excess that it was already gone?

"Quite a lot to keep a man busy here," Armand commented. "I fear the grounds will never be just right."

"But they are exquisite, Alexandre," Madeleine couldn't help but reply. "I've been nothing but stunned since arriving. You simply must escort me through the gardens and explain your work. I admit I'm quite an admirer of carved shrubbery. The lines are so precise, as if carved from stone, yet they breathe a life of their own. I adore them."

Armand cast her a quizzical look, accompanied by a sneaking smile. "Shrubbery, eh?"

"I've always adored shrubs." Well, not exactly. But a few moments in Alexandre's company, so she might pick his brain regarding his brother would be most helpful in her endeavors.

"Interesting. Ah, but if I left you to my brother's attentions regarding his plants, then he'll have you for the entire afternoon. Perhaps we could locate our rooms first?" He gifted her with a purely wanton look.

Madeleine's heart fluttered as his dark orbs ensorceled her into a hankering to submit. Right now. Right here. "Indeed? Oh yes, our rooms! First. Of course!"

She snapped out of her dumbfounded state. She was the one supposedly doing the seducing, not him! The roles of pretender had been exchanged in her favor. But for some reason he was always one length ahead of her.

"Alexandre, perhaps I could return for a tour after we've settled in?"

"I'll be waiting."

The brothers bid each other *au revoir,* and Madeleine waved the couple away, quite aware that Sophie sulked with arms crossed over her chest.

As they watched the twosome stroll up the wide center alley of raked stone to the steps of the main château, Alexandre couldn't help but be thrilled for his brother. Finally, he had found someone. At least he hoped Armand had found someone. Someone who would make a difference in his life, ground him with the kind of love that could make a man forget his criminal past. "I like her."

Sophie snorted from behind him. "You've just met her."

"She's very pretty."

"I don't like her."

Of course Sophie would not.

"She's just too . . . too . . . tall. That's it. Dreadful how she almost tops Armand's height, isn't it? And that hair. All this way and that. Those big curls are quite unfashionable—"

"Sophie."

"Yes, love?"

Alexandre still followed the retreating duo with his eyes. "Do tend our children, will you?"

Armand leaned against the wall in the bedchamber he'd been directed to by a lackey after explaining he had come to visit his brother and—wink, wink—holiday with the beauty at his side.

Everything was a deep forest green, from the bedding to the exotic carpets dotted in gold fleur-de-lis, to the velvet-tufted cushions on the dark walnut chairs. Overhead, a wide crystal chandelier sparkled, seeming to virtually bloom from the ceiling mural of a pastoral scene. Fresh flowers bloomed in massive silver urns in two corners of the room. Where they had come from was a mystery. Unless there were flower gardens behind the château especially for cutting?

Everywhere gold sparkled; in the arabesques of velvet covering the walls, in the mural fluttering across the ceiling, in the fabrics. The chairs and table and even the boiseries were of gold. It was as if they'd stepped inside a treasure chest. Whether it was real, or merely gild, Armand would soon determine.

Madeleine's attention had been captured by a blanket laid across the foot of the bed. Thick midnight velvet dotted with soft rosettes of crimson velvet, and fringed in fat twisted cords of even more gold.

Quite luxurious for bed dressings, Armand noted. Indeed, if this were a mere guest room, Fouquet certainly had spared no expense. But whose expense was the bill tallied under?

Armand adjusted his weight, switching feet. Madeleine had spread herself across the foot of the bed. The wide spray of her violet skirts did not hide her satin slippers and ankles. Thin cream stockings decorated with red clocks clung to her narrow limbs.

Delicious.

Her fingers glided admiringly over the velvet rosettes, her intentions perhaps as confused as his own. She wasn't thinking of fabric or its design. She could not be for the lingering rhythm her fingers traced over the velvet. As if she were studying a man's flesh . . .

A sudden vision of himself appeared, lying at the foot of the bed, his chest bared to Madeleine's delicate fingers as she tripped her nails across his hardened nipples. Fireflashes danced across her face and rippled in her curls. Temptation surrounded her like a djinni's mist.

Armand snapped his eyes shut and drew in a heavy breath. Pacing. Seduction requires pacing. Know your prey as . . . *she knows you?* He blinked at this revelation.

"Something has occured to me."

"Yes?" Bewitching, her gaze. Syrupy, her voice.

Steel yourself, Saint-Sylvestre.

"I realize this was a ploy to attain a husband for his daughter, but how can your father be so quick to jump into the fire? He knows nothing about me. I am just a stranger the two of you plucked out of a crowd. Or am I?"

He caught her nervous blink. But she recovered quickly. "Madame, how many secrets do you possess?" he murmured to himself.

"Of course you are, Armand." She drew out the last syllable of his name as if she were pressing her tongue against the sound, tasting it, possessing it.

"Which brings me to the question of how you knew my name. You cannot tell me there was not extensive forethought regarding last night's fiasco. Can you?"

The blanket forgotten, Madeleine straightened and glanced aside. The play of afternoon sun across her face softened her hair into a mix of precious metals: gold, copper, and bronze. She seemed quite aware of his intensity. He knew she hid something.

And she knew that he knew.

But now to see how she would play things.

"We, er . . . asked around after spying you. I shouldn't exactly use the word spy—"

Armand tensed.

"—more like, noticed. Papa saw that you were speaking to the captain of the guards. You dress very well, kept good company, and he knew you would be honorable if not trustworthy. And I . . . well . . . I found your appearance rather to my liking." She flashed him a brief smile and flickering lashes. "But you are correct, I know nothing of you." Again, she met his eyes quickly, then looked to the floor.

Interesting play. Who was the real pretender here?

Deep in his gut Armand had the feeling that something was not right. But what exactly? Intuition had saved his hide many a time. But this time it was behaving like an elusive fox.

"Why would you believe I am nothing but the rogue I claim to be?"

"I've no reason to believe otherwise. But you make it sound an evil thing."

"My lady, the tone of your voice shivers beneath your brave words. You want me, but at the same time you fear what I might be."

"Nonsense! I have no fear of you. *Rogue* is merely an exotic label placed upon men who don't fall under the usual category of gentleman or fop. In fact, I find *rogue* to be rather intriguing."

Indeed she would. A fiery woman, his Madame Medusa.

Just what Armand craved most, too—fire.

But there was something beneath the surface that kept her flame from igniting into a blaze. What that was might possibly be an overbearing father who demanded she heed his bidding. Or was it something else that made Madeleine hold back?

"Come here." She patted the blanket beside her.

On the other hand, she did put delicious effort into the fanning of her flames. Perhaps he'd not yet tapped into the spark that simmered just beneath the surface. She possessed control. A control that teased Armand to try to loosen its grip.

Instead of sitting where she wished, Armand leaned over her, forcing her prone across the thickly quilted counterpane and fencing her on either side with his arms. He hovered above her, fighting the bewitchery that brewed in her eyes. "A rogue might be unsavory and evil. A criminal even. Perhaps I am such a criminal."

She touched his shirt, toyed with the ties at his neck. Amber caressed his senses. This is not what he wanted. He wanted to see doubt in her eyes. A moment of fear. Only then would he have the upper hand, which was necessary. Always.

He snatched her fingers and squeezed them firmly. "Don't you believe me, Madeleine? If I say I am a criminal, then I must be."

"Why would a criminal confess?"

"I could rob a man of his purse, seduce the jewels from a woman's neck."

"Seduce me," she cooed.

While his conscience screamed how wrong this whole situation was, the connection between him and Madeleine felt oddly . . . right. And that frightened Armand more than the prospect of hanging in the gallows for his past crimes.

He could not deny this charade of husband and wife proved no merit beyond the possible challenge to his emotions. Which would indeed be a pricey challenge to match. For to tap into his long-pent-up emotions promised to be too painful even to consider.

Armand pulled her to him and smoothed a hand aside her cheek, forcing her to meet his gaze. "You require seduction? But I think it is you that claims the title of seductress, Madame Medusa. Listen. Shh . . . I can hear your snakes hissing."

She kissed him. Slowly. Softly. Once, and then twice. The wily seductress had seeped into her eyes and voice. "And do my hisses tempt you?" A kiss to his earlobe startled. His body stiffened with need. "I've captured you, now let me play with my prey before it escapes. *S'il vous plaît?*"

Whatever fantasy she imagined . . . Armand was all for feeding it. Especially when his body ached for satisfaction. But he wasn't about to let her win this round.

"Once again you've succeeded in turning me hard as stone, Medusa. Feel the result of your powers, my wicked seductress."

He pulled her hand down and pressed it against his erection.

The flash in her eyes pleased him. *Touché.* He could set her off the course of her seductions as easily as she could him. She flinched, but he would not allow her to pull away. "You don't want to play anymore?"

A knock at the door stopped them both. Armand whispered a hissing oath and sprang from the bed, while he distinctly heard Madeleine's sigh as he approached the door.

A sigh of relief? Most surely. He'd called her bluff. Ha-ha!

"Ah, Alexandre, the man with impeccable timing."

Madeleine shuffled to the edge of the bed and adjusted her hair. The heat of her embarrassment quickened in her cheeks and décolletage so deliciously Armand was all for slamming the door in his brother's face and claiming her right here and now.

"Forgive me, brother." Alexandre started cautiously at the sight of Madeleine slipping from the bed. "Perhaps I should have waited for the two of you to come to me. Sophie has seen the children in for their naps, and I've the rest of the afternoon for leisure. That is until the gilded tubs of orange trees arrive."

"Gilded?" Armand noted.

"For the fête. Fouquet has demanded nothing but the finest for the king."

"Of course."

Madeleine observed Armand's acquiescent acceptance of his brother's statement. As he smoothed a finger across his stubbled chin, his dark eyes deep in thought, she couldn't help wonder what he was thinking. That "of course," hadn't been a normal "of course." It had hinted of suspicion. As any good spy should be suspect. But why the interest in gilded planting pots? Had he plans to steal from Fouquet? Why else the interest in the value of things around the estate?

Hmm, she must report this to Fouquet immediately.

"You go with Alexandre." Armand pulled her from her musing with a nod of his head. "I'll join you in a moment."

"But we can wait," she said. "What have you to do?"

Gripping the door with a tight fist, Armand summoned an excuse. "I need to wash up after the journey here. Run along, Madeleine, you might seek out the statuary. Perhaps there's a figure of Medusa and one of her stone-bodied victims?"

Stone-bodied, eh? He'd startled her by laying her hand over his loins. The man had been absolutely rigid under her palm. Perhaps . . . could he still be?

She glanced at his breeches, but he stood at an odd angle in the doorway, his hip to her, the ribboned rosettes dusting his doublet covering what she most wanted to see. She knew the connection of their bodies had been the reason he'd become so aroused.

But how now, would he become *un*aroused? Would it remain stiff forever? Oh, but that had to be awkward!

"Mademoiselle?"

Madeleine glanced at Alexandre's hooked arm and hopeful "come-along-then" expression.

"Run along, darling."

"If you're sure?"

Though, perhaps she didn't want to know how he would deal with the situation. Not in the presence of his brother. A few minutes to wash up and then he'd be at her side?

"Very well." She hooked an arm in Alexandre's, but remained fixed to Armand's smiling face. He was up to something; she sensed it. And it had nothing to do with the height of his arousal either.

This would be the first time a female had left Armand Saint-Sylvestre high and dry. Not by her own choosing, though. So Armand was inclined not to give Madeleine points for such a move.

Now that he had successfully seen Madeleine away from his side, business called. He had, since he'd been forced to ride the road, been in some of France's finest châteaux. Armand knew luxury, and he also knew faux luxury. Dukes and barons who had lost a family fortune due to gambling or wenching would cover only the public walls in their homes with English paper and faux-gilded boiserie, leaving their private chambers bare-walled and cold because they hadn't the proper finances to do them up right. Widows left with nothing but empty rooms and the haunting laughter of their departed's knowing, would sell their jewels and replace them with paste in order to retain their standing in society.

Ah, but genuine luxury seeped through the walls and clung in the air like a heavy perfume that seduces a man into hallucinations of grandeur. And as he walked the halls of Vaux that perfume stirred in Armand's head.

Not a single portion of wall, ceiling, or floor, had not been coated with damask and silk, gilded wood or carved silver fir. The fixtures on the doors and candelabra were gold. Solid gold. Armand wondered with disdain what King Louis would think of such blatant extravagance. It was no secret the king had had to melt down his own gold serviceware and settings to defray the last remaining expenses following that damned war that had mustered through three decades.

Beneath his boots marble flowed like a calm ocean in multiveined colors that defied nature. The window dressings were, at closer inspection, heavy damask shot through with silver threads and lined in a rich silk that would never be seen save by the sun's fading rays. Chandeliers constellated everywhere, sprinkling from the ceiling like so many sprays of falling stars.

It was impossible to believe that any man, save a king, could afford such trappings. Even a king would have to ransom his country to purchase the paintings that hung on the walls. Le Brun's signature arabesqued a good many paintings, his vivid brushstrokes graced even the murals on the ceilings. Masters from decades past such as Mignard, Titian and—was that a

Raphael?—decorated the walls with their rich oils and solemn colors.

A marble statue of a man's torso tempted Armand to touch the muscled arm. One of Madame Medusa's victims? He smiled at the thought. How stone could be coaxed into such smoothness—it seemed to even breathe life—was beyond him. Give him a chisel and hammer and the statue's torso would be seriously disfigured. He would leave the art to the masters.

Though the possession of such art had once been his trade. Nothing as large as this statue. No, mostly small objects d'art and jewelry. Armand could price a sparkling strand of gemstones from across a ballroom, and plot the abduction of the piece by the time he'd broached the wearer with a charming smile and a whisper of late-night seductions.

Women were so easily seduced.

So why did it seem as though Madeleine was mastering this game of seduction? He just couldn't get the upper hand.

He leaned against the wall, crossing his arms over his chest. Why did he need the upper hand? This was not a plot for him to master and conquer. He served the king now, not himself. Madeleine was merely a diversion, a trifle to be tolerated until the mission was complete.

And that was why he was so vexed!

He no longer had the desire to seduce and conquer, yet Madeleine's very presence demanded his attention, his touches, his kisses. The old thrill had returned. The fire he sought simmered within his grasp.

Certainly the woman was attractive; not to be turned away by any man. But Armand knew well enough that he could have dashed away from the priest's demands for compliance at that moment of catastrophe when Papa had fainted and all about had been chaos.

So why hadn't he? He was too smart for such a ruse.

Too smart when he used his brain, that is.

The only time Armand had ever found himself caring for a

woman beyond the desire for her riches was when he'd been listening to his heart. And that had only happened once before. And he was paying for it dearly now.

Ah! In little less than twenty-four hours, marriage to the fire-haired Medusa had caused Armand no amount of distraction. Of course he might easily think there was something more to this new alliance when he'd been worked over by her bewitchery. She merely needed him to please her father. A bargain had been struck. His relationship with Madeleine was nothing but business.

Time to start thinking with his brain again.

"Back to work."

Armand knocked quietly at the door. No answer, so he carefully eased the door open and slipped inside, taking care to leave the door propped open an inch so he could listen for curious servants. Though he'd seen only the one lackey who had brought him and Madeleine to their room, perhaps the others were occupied with party arrangements.

The room was small, made even more so by the rows of wood shelving that lined the walls. On each shelf were scads of perfectly spaced artifacts. Upon closer observation, Armand found they were tiny porcelain figures. Delicate boxes in whimsical shapes, which, when opened, revealed a prize in relation to the design of the outer box.

A pink party cake opened to reveal a gold-wrapped present, the entire assemblage no bigger than his fist. Worth one hundred livres, to be sure. A green-eyed cat opened to reveal a mouse. A tapestry sewing box revealed needle and thread exquisitely carved in the delicate porcelain. Next to that sat a most curious creation. A woman's skirt pulled to reveal her legs mid-thigh.

Armand leaned against a windowpane to study the intricate creation, but found his attention was drawn to the front grounds, where his brother's handiwork curled into a sort of emerald-and-rust quilt design.

She was easy enough to spot in the subdued violet skirts,

but it was really the vibrant red hair that caught Armand's eye. Her head tilted back in laughter, Madeleine pressed a hand to her breast as Alexandre made some gesture up the length of a conical yew topiary.

Though the windowpane blocked all sound of her mirth, Armand could feel her happiness vibrate in his heart; her smile coaxed the corners of his mouth to curve upward. What Alexandre could be talking about, he hadn't a clue. Might be something as mundane as plant genus or trimming procedures. But it was when Madeleine stretched her arms wide and literally hugged the shrub that Armand's heart pulsed a quick double beat.

"Hugging shrubs, eh? The woman really does have a fetish for the plants. Strange." Even as he mouthed the word he also felt a warm flush of enchantment heat his heart. And he thought he heard a gentle rapping, somewhere . . .

Tap, tap.

Armand pressed a hand to his chest. There was that odd sound again. He'd heard it once before, at Versailles, when his fate had so precariously marched a fragile line. Whatever could that be? It had not been an audible sound. More like, it had come from . . . within?

He listened again. Nothing.

Ah well.

Outside, Madeleine released the shrub and bussed Alexandre's cheeks with quick kisses, then spun toward the stone walk. Off to seduce another topiary?

Armand snickered as his brother disappeared behind the bushes.

"You never stop, do you Alexandre," he commented of his brother's endless quest for work.

Of course, the fact that his wife was Sophie could have quite a bit to do with his brother's staunch work ethic. Sophie Marie Saint-Sylvestre. Now that was a mouthful any man would do well to avoid. Pity, Alexandre was so kindhearted. Armand

would never allow himself to fall for a woman's pouting lips
and . . .

Ah hell! *Forget this nonsense,* Armand said to himself. *Don't
think of lips or kisses or batting eyelashes, it'll only vex you
further!*

"Did you get lost on your way to the garden?"

The voice startled Armand so thoroughly that the porcelain
legs slipped from his fingers. As he frantically fumbled to
secure hold, the elusive object bounced from one clumsy finger,
into the air, and bounced off another clumsily placed finger.
Finally, he swooped both hands and caught the fragile piece
against his chest.

Fury tightening his brow, Armand turned to find Madeleine
standing behind him, her smile irrepressible after witnessing
his dance with the breakable object.

"What are you doing here? You were just—" *Hugging
shrubs. Enticing me to study you. Causing my heart to do
strange things.*

"I should ask you the same," she countered, hooking one
hand on her hip. With her other hand she pried his fingers from
his chest and plucked out the porcelain. She tipped the box top
open to reveal the inner treasure. "Interesting."

"I got lost." He set the piece on the shelf and pushed Madeleine toward the door. "It's a huge estate. I couldn't recall
whether to turn left or right as I exited our room."

"Left would have taken you to the door less than ten strides
away and right out into the gardens. What are you up to,
husband dearest?"

"I've already told you. I've a mission."

"Yes, yes, but what sort of mission would find a foot soldier
poking about the finance minister's private estate?"

Finesse she did not possess. What concern was it of hers
what he did with himself? Intuition skirted through Armand's
system. But again, it was so fleeting a feeling he just couldn't
grasp it.

"Didn't Alexandre have anything of interest to show you? What about Sophie; perhaps the two of you might get along."

"Oh yes, and an Englishman should invite a Frenchman to dine on frog-leg soufflé."

"Now what's wrong with Sophie?"

"She doesn't like me."

"The two of you barely spoke one word to another."

"Exactly. Did you see the looks she gave me when we arrived?" She crossed her eyes in comical mockery, causing Armand to chuckle. "I'm surprised my flesh has not burned from my bones."

Hooking his arm around Madeleine's waist, Armand led the two of them toward the guest room. "The woman does have a rather wicked way about her. Gives me the chills just being in the same room with her."

Madeleine's skirts swished against Armand's ankles as they walked. If he'd been wearing buckled shoes, he might have felt the silk slide across his calves. For once Armand cursed his need to wear boots.

"Alexandre seems such a gentle, soft-spoken man," she said. "Sophie is a hardened socialite whom I wager could spot a stray hair mussed in a coif from across a ballroom. It's hard to imagine two more opposite people."

"My brother was trapped into marriage."

Armand paused, and Madeleine walked a few paces more before stopping and spinning toward him, sudden anxiety widening her eyes. "What do you mean?"

I guess it runs in the family. Until that very moment, Armand had not even thought to compare his situation with his brother's. How odd that two in the same family should fall upon the same fate.

He saw trepidation flash in Madeleine's eyes. "I don't wish you to hold this unfortunate situation against me. Oh, please Armand, you know I was only trying to please my father."

"You needn't worry. It's not as though I will be in this situation for much longer."

He walked on, leaving her to follow if she chose. Her skirts did not begin their muted swishing. When Armand reached the outer door, he did not turn around. He'd stymied her with his confession regarding Alexandre's marriage. Good. The woman needed a little shaking up.

And he needed to keep his mind on business.

Seven

The idea of meandering about the gardens with Armand and his brother, knowing what she now knew of their unfortunate love affairs, did not sit well with Madeleine. Instead she used Armand's absence to compose a note to Valérie.

Her cousin must never know the base level to which Madeleine had sunk to preserve her own wealth on Stephan's behalf. Nor must Valérie know that her uncle suspected a spy in his midst. Fouquet had made it quite clear his niece must never learn of Madeleine's involvement with him. But Madeleine saw no harm in writing to tell Valérie she was vacationing at Vaux. It would perhaps cheer her up.

Another note was quickly penned to assure Fouquet she'd successfully insinuated herself into Armand's life. She still knew little to nothing about Armand's mission, but included a few lines about his attention to the finer things at Vaux. Madeleine could almost see the mental calculations of cost scrolling in Armand's head as he took in his surroundings.

"She lives in the Marais on the Rue de Bearn," Madeleine

directed the gangly teen whom she'd found mucking the stables. "The other will find Monsieur Fouquet at the Louvre."

Waving the beaming youngster off, Madeleine crossed her fingers behind her back. She prayed return word would find Valérie much improved. Though against all hopes, she knew in her heart there was but one fate for her cousin.

To think that her son might soon be an orphan. Why, Stephan was but four months old. He would never be given the opportunity to know a mother's hugs and kisses. He deserved better.

And wouldn't Madeleine love to give him everything he needed. She looked forward to mothering Stephan, to granting him a mother like she had never had herself.

Plucking up her mask, she headed outside in search of her errant spy. A wide stone path led from the main château to the stables.

Madeleine was gaining ground in the intimacy department. That was the easy part of her task. Every touch, every look Armand granted her was a delicious poison that she couldn't decide whether to taste or cast away. Her body pleaded for a grand feast, but her mind still struggled with right and wrong.

"*I* could easily fall in love with him."

He was very handsome, tall and strong. That face, perfectly honed from an artist's mind. The looks he gave her. It was as if he touched her every time, in a different, yet delicious place. And that voice. She closed her eyes to re-create his husky voice in her mind. Commanding if need be, enticing and pleading when in her arms.

Madeleine had always wanted love. Dreamed of being noticed, of feeling special. It had been difficult growing up at court. Her mother had been devoted to the duchess, trailing Her Grace's skirt hem from sunup to sundown, while Madeleine played with the other children. Well, tried to play. It was a rare day that would pass without the usual teasing. She wasn't royalty, not fit to eat from their serviceware, nor to enter the royal gardens and play. And look at that hair and all those freckles! Devil's marks. Witch, witch, they'd taunt, if she came within teasing range. Which had been rare as well. Instead she had lingered in the shadows, hoping upon hope to wake one morning with plain brown hair and smooth, flawless skin. Just once.

But once she'd grown out of her awkward pubescent years and had learned the art of disguising her freckles with face cream, Madeleine had no problem in attracting suitors. Only they were all fops. Powdered and curled, pompous fops. Including her late husband. Not one of them knew the real meaning of love, of being *in* love. Nor had any of them a clue as to how to hold a woman so she might lose all control over her legs and literally fall into his arms.

Armand Saint-Sylvestre could do that. And he needn't even touch her. A mere look from his ebony eyes was all it took. *Right here,* she recalled the words he'd spoken last night as he'd directed her into his eyes. *This is where you belong.*

To belong somewhere, anywhere, but most especially—in his eyes.

What a dream.

Madeleine wondered now if Armand possessed the compassion and patience to make a good father. Stephan would certainly thrive with a man such as Armand to guide him from infant skirts to a strapping young man destined for a great future.

"Oh, Madeleine, are you falling victim to this man's affections?"

She knew that any emotion Armand expressed toward her could only be an act. A well-honed act that he'd practiced for years on unsuspecting widows. Whether it was a conscious decision or not, he could only be toying with her now. As for even considering the notion of he playing a father to Valérie's son—ah!—she was certainly losing her senses.

One way or another this charade would come to an end. And that end would see her alone again.

"Enjoy the moment," she whispered. "While you can."

Evening silenced the shouts of workers erecting the fir stage behind the château and settled a welcome quiet upon the entire grounds. A great bonfire burned to the east of the estate, where the workers had camped in gypsy wagons and carriages; some even slept beneath the open sky.

Madeleine meandered in a slow circle about the grounds just below her chamber window. Armand had yet to show, and the evening meal had not yet been delivered to her room, so she decided to venture outside where wafts of roast pork curled through the air and tickled her nose.

The grass was cool on her bare feet, and her skirts sang a sweet melody as they skimmed the wide base of a conical topiary. She touched the surface of the carved shrub, remembering Alexandre's explanation of how he made sure each tree's design was geometrically exact by use of ropes and stones to form a cage about the plant. As he snipped, the ropes became a guide.

"Hugging shrubbery again, I see."

"Armand." He stood against the curved stone archway that led into the gardens behind the château, his legs crossed at the ankle and both arms laced over his chest. A crisp Holland shirt ribboned below his elbows and round his wrists, and he wore his hair loose now. His boots blended with the shadows, and the glint of sword was absent from his side.

"You sneak about very well, you know that?"

He shrugged and offered a proud grin. Or maybe a knowing grin.

"And you tend to take your love for shrubbery to the extreme, Madame. Tell me, do you often hug trees?"

"As often as possible," she teased with a coy wink of her

lashes. Trickling her fingers down the angle of scratchy yew, she countered, "This shrub needs love as much as anything else."

"It is an inanimate object."

"A living thing that takes well to your brother's loving touch. How resplendent the grounds are because of his attentions."

"So you've taken to offering them your own attentions? Pity such affections are wasted on the shrubs and not myself."

"I've granted you much affection, Monsieur. Perhaps it is only because you were nowhere in sight, and I was feeling rather ignored—"

His movement was stealthy and swift. Madeleine found herself in Armand's arms. A nice place to be. The pressure of his hand, centered upon her spine and just fitting against her lower back, moved her forward to fit against his body. His other hand held hers out to the side, as if to begin a curious dance step.

The clasp of his fingers around hers spoke of possession. The look in his eyes repeated the bewitching mantra . . . "Right here, here is where you belong."

In his eyes.

"You, Monsieur"—she gasped as his fingertips caressed her spine, his thumb curved commandingly around her waist, his eyes holding her riveted—"certainly know how to hold a woman."

He winked and began to tilt her backward.

"What are you doing?" she asked.

"I want to show you something."

"What?" As she became parallel with the ground, his sure grip did not lessen, nor did his fingers dig into her flesh as if he were straining to hold her. She was his puppet, following his command of her strings. And she did not feel one ounce of fear that he might tangle them or drop her in a heap.

"Look up into the sky," he said, his piercing gaze studying hers. "Do you see it? Can you touch them?"

It was if someone had punched tiny holes in a dark canvas

and placed it before a candle flame to allow the golden warmth to flicker through. Madeleine extended a hand and grasped the air. "I wish I could touch one."

"But you can. You may even hold one if you wish."

"How? Oh, show me, please."

He straightened, bringing her up with him. Always in his eyes, and ever his willing captive. But he must never know he could have—and quite possibly *did* have—the upper hand in this relationship.

"Do this." He held one arm up and extended his fingers, wiggling them in example.

Madeleine did the same.

"Now, turn your hand away from you and place it over that star. Yes, that large one that shines so brightly."

As she extended her reach and moved her palm over the large star, Armand stepped behind her and Madeleine felt his arms slip around her waist. The heat of his breath hushed near her ear. The desire in her heart pulsed faster.

"Now snap your fingers shut and don't move. You've captured it."

"I have! I've caught a star in my hand."

"And I've its mistress in my arms."

His gentle nibbling at her ear sparked a surge of elation throughout Madeleine's being. Arm still extended, and star firmly in grasp, she tilted her head to the side to coax Armand's explorations. He found the sensitive flesh of her neck. Heat prickled in her bosom and cheeks and shot the spark down to her waist, where his hands had claimed her.

"I fear I may let go of my star," she managed, though at the moment stars held no interest for her.

"You may release it, but from here on you shall forever be its mistress. Lucky star."

Pulling her arm down, Madeleine turned in Armand's embrace. Yes, it was easy, succumbing to this man's charms. Yes, she craved this feeling of being wanted, of being adored.

Oh, that the world was becoming a most conflicting place. To continue this act or to surrender to her desire?

"I want you to kiss me." She pressed a finger to his lips as he eagerly took to her command. "Wait. First, I want you to forget why we are together. Forget everything about last night. I just want to be a woman and a man, standing under the starshine, no agreements or deception tainting our emotions."

"I would like that very much."

So did she. Now . . . dare she ask it? Yes, she must! "I want you to kiss me, as—as if you loved me."

He paused, his lips but a breath away from hers. Resignation steeped in his tone. "I'm afraid I cannot do that, Madame, for that sort of kiss I am not privy to."

Her hopes deflated.

"You see, I've never known love, so I've yet to know how to kiss in love," he added.

"Oh."

"Forgive me."

She was about to say, "That's quite all right. I've asked for far too much."

But he spoke instead. "Close your eyes, Madeleine."

Simple enough request.

She relaxed and let darkness fall over her vision. The touch of his lips to her left eyelid felt soft as a garden rabbit's nuzzle. He held there, imbuing her flesh with the imprint of his mouth, steady, gentle, so full of life. Then he moved to kiss her other eyelid. Slow. Warm. So stunningly sensuous that Madeleine had to mentally communicate with her knees not to bend and pull her down and away from his attentions.

When he finally pulled back, she read the message in his eyes. *I want to love you. I really do.* No other interpretation could be decided but that. He just didn't know how to love. Perhaps he'd played the game of seduction for so long, he could never know how.

She would teach him. Somehow.

Slipping her fingers into his hand, Madeleine pulled up close and whispered, "That was a good start, Armand."

"Ah . . . what have I started?"

"I've never felt more loved in my entire life."

Her comment seemed to surprise, even startle him. But Armand quickly recovered, sweeping his fingers over his jaw and rubbing his lips. "I shall remember that. Er, for future reference."

"Of course."

No, he wasn't yet ready to surrender to his feelings. But soon. She hoped.

"Shall we?" He gestured to the château, and Madeleine followed him across the walk that bridged the moat and inside.

She'd caught him off guard just now as he'd struggled for a response to her statement.

Armand did have a soft spot. It was the unearthing of his own emotions.

A late meal of roast pork stuffed with dates and smothered in wine sauce waited in their shared bedchamber. Vaux boasted two chefs, a pastry specialist, and a wine master, but Madeleine suspected tonight's meal might have been courtesy of the worker's pig roast, with a few extra touches. Delighted also to find that someone had drawn a bath in the adjoining chamber, Madeleine pleaded indulgence over warm food.

Half an hour later she wore a soft white robe embroidered in tiny red roses with arabesques of emerald vining. Tapers had been lit upon the table and the armoire, and deep burgundy wine had been poured.

Armand stood waiting by her chair, shirtsleeves tugged up to his elbows as if he'd finished a day's labor, and hair free of a ribbon. She couldn't imagine the man ever looking anything less than devastating. It was easy to understand now how he might have used his charm to steal. What woman could resist such allure?

"Fit for a king," she commented, as Armand held out a chair and seated her at the dining table intimately sized for two.

Madeleine placed a morsel of pork on the tip of her tongue. It was tangy and moist at first, replaced by the subtle moody bite of mushroom wine sauce. Delicious. Though, she was used to court food. Leftovers. It had been a rare day in her childhood to receive warm food, unless she slipped into the galley and sneaked a taste here and there while the cooks hadn't been looking.

"Perhaps a king's first course." He sipped the wine, then teased his minuscule portion of pork with the tip of a silver knife. "Though I'd wager the dining ware and plates to be solid silver. They're quite hefty."

"Why are you so concerned with the expense of Vaux's offerings? You've not missed tallying a single item since arriving. If I did not know better," she continued her mode of inquiry, "I should suspect you've an eye for fine things."

Armand looked up from his goblet of wine. When he placed the shimmering crystal on the table he smoothed his palms over the damask table covering. "Is there anything wrong with appreciating fine things?"

"Not at all. But from what you've told me you are hardly a man of high station."

"Must one be of high station to desire extravagance?"

"Certainly not. I just meant—well, you don't seem the sort to be lured by wealth or fine things." Another bite. "Are you?"

"Am I what?"

Much as she knew the answer, she had to prod. "Lured by riches?"

"Not of the material sort."

"What other sort is there?"

"As you can see," he said, a dash of seduction deepening his voice, "I've acquired a most fine wife."

Madeleine felt her cheeks flush, her breasts swell with arousal. No, she could not lose to desire now. Not when she'd started on a path to discovery. She must keep Fouquet satisfied and, in turn, keep de Pellison at bay.

"From what you've told me of your mission I have difficulty judging the final goal. You are here on your own?"

"By my employer's request."

"Ah." Interesting. Armand had not come of his own volition. So that would certainly rule out stealing, wouldn't it? Perhaps not. "And what is it your employer wants of this mission?"

"It is not what my employer wants so much as what Fouquet has taken."

A third bite of pork stalled in Madeleine's throat.

"I can say nothing more." Armand made haste of his portion of roast. He'd spoken more than he wished, it was plain in his actions now.

Fouquet had stolen something? She'd only once met the man and had found him to work charm to a deadly advantage. He was rumored to be an excellent financier, very close to the king. If Fouquet suspected Armand of spying—

Did Armand spy on Fouquet because the financier was suspected of stealing?

Did *she* work for a criminal?

No, it had to be something entirely different. Perhaps whatever Fouquet had taken was not a tangible thing. Maybe it had something to do with Armand's employer. Who could that possibly be?

"You do not find the meal to your liking?"

She glanced to Armand's clean plate. He'd refilled his goblet and sluiced its fragrant contents over his lips. "Hmm? Oh, the meal. Yes, I do find it quite tasty. I was just thinking."

"About?"

About all manner of criminal deeds, including her own

venture into deception. While she was doing this to ensure
the future of a small child, she must also acknowledge that
she would be harming Armand. Well . . . surely he does
deserve to pay for his past crimes. But never a swing in the
gallows. Certainly such a fate should not befall this handsome
man.

His employer had sent him here to discover a crime of
Fouquet's?

"More thoughts?" he prompted.

"Hmm? Oh, yes." So he was not here on a criminal mission.

"Roast or riches?" he wondered, setting his elbows on the
table and leaning across his plate to study her more closely.
"I'd say definitely not food."

"Armand." She couldn't escape the dark thoughts that suddenly reared in her mind. Who was the real criminal in this
little adventure? Armand? Fouquet? Or her? "Have you ever
done something . . ." She toyed with the heavy silver knife,
finding her appetite had fled. "Something you knew might be
wrong, perhaps even criminal, but would benefit someone you
cared for with all your heart?"

"Deep thoughts for roast and wine." He studied her through
the hypnotic flicker of amber candle flame. "Where did that
come from?"

"Oh, I don't know. Just a thought really."

"What have you done wrong, Madeleine?"

"You mean besides tricking you into marriage? You know
that's what I was thinking about. But I do believe it did some
benefit to Papa. I've written to Les Invalides. I feel sure he
will recover now to know—or at least to believe—that I am
happy."

Yet another lie so easily doled out. What was becoming of
her morals? Would the end result really be worth her abandon-
ment of all that was right?

"But what about you? Have you ever betrayed one to serve
another?"

His abrupt departure from the table stirred up a wind that flickered the candle to a spiral of gray smoke. She'd hit a nerve. Not intentionally—her own thoughts had just lent to the mood. But this entrance into Armand's psyche was not to be refused.

Madeleine rushed to him as he paced to the door opposite the bed and worked the crystal knob. He toed the base of the door, not planning to open it, but not wanting to turn to face her either.

She touched his shoulder. He tilted his head back. Curls as dark as black glass slipped over her fingers. As dark as his thoughts?

"What have you done, Armand?"

"Nothing."

"You can tell me, I would understand." Yes, she did want to understand what little she knew of his past. How he did it, why he did it. *If* he still served his need for stolen riches. "You know, we are the same."

He spun round and gripped her arms, his eyes ebony bullets aiming for her heart. "We are not the same, Madeleine. We are different as red and black. You are bright and beautiful, while I . . . I have no reason to be proud of my past."

"What of your past?"

"I cannot talk about this."

"You have something to be ashamed of?"

The jerk of his head might be construed as a positive nod, but it was so fleeting, she dared not label it so. Rather, she didn't *want* to label it as such, even knowing that it could be nothing but.

"My past is not your concern, Madame. Now . . ." He turned the knob and opened the door to another room.

Madeleine spied the tester bed inside the darkened room, turned down for tonight's occupants. "Who's staying in there?"

"I am." He walked over the threshold and stood facing her,

two opponents separated by an invisible line. "I thought it necessary considering the circumstances."

"But—"

He thrust up a placating hand. "I have no intention of forgetting our agreement. Believe me"—his eyes raked her over, lingering on her bosom, too well covered by the heavy robe— "that will never slip my mind. But don't you think it entirely too easy confining us both to the same room?"

"Well . . ." Not necessarily.

She reached out but could not touch him without stepping over the threshold that worked as some odd barrier that, for some inexplicable reason, she respected. "I want you to stay with me tonight."

"You want me?" He tilted his head in an intriguing summation and she became caught in his eyes. *Where she belonged.*

"I do."

A ridiculously smug smile curved onto his lips. "Well . . . you can't have me. Yet."

And he closed the door.

Eight

Madeleine pressed her palms against the door, flattening them as if there were a way to divine his presence through the barrier. "Armand?"

"Yes?"

She could hear his voice as plainly as if he stood with the door open. But unable to see his expression, to know he held her in his eyes, stymied her to a vexing consternation. Much as she wanted to, she resisted stomping her foot.

"What is wrong? What have I done to deserve this sequestration from you?"

"Not a thing." A slight pressure against the door thrummed against Madeleine's palms. He had propped a shoulder against the door, or perhaps stood with his back to it. "I merely believe it wise to prolong the seduction a bit longer. What would be the thrill of *anything* with such instant gratification?"

Besides the fact it would then grant them time to do it again and again and again before this whole scam was complete?

"You've changed your mind, I know it." Madeleine pressed her forehead to the door.

She'd had him, in her hands, but she'd been too forward. He was retreating from her advances like a deer stalked by a lioness. So much power she'd wielded in her kisses. And she not even aware of it!

Unless . . .

"So I've frightened the master of seduction off with my own power of charm? Have my snakes made you retreat?"

"Never."

"Appears quite that way, you standing behind a locked door, and poor little me, unarmed . . ."

"Unarmed? Ha! I think it is you Mademoiselle—"

"Madame."

"Yes, Madame—it is you that may be slipping. Afraid you cannot wait? Do you need me so desperately that you fear you'll fall before me and ransom your virtue with nothing but a breath?"

Yes. But it was her virtue that had become a commodity lately. One she had to guard from falling into the wrong hands. Though, by no means would she put Armand Saint-Sylvestre on the *wrong* list.

"I can last far longer than you, Monsieur Saint-Sylvestre." Speaking the words straightened her resolve, as well as her shoulders.

"We'll see about that, Madame Saint-Sylvestre."

"Allow me to fend off your best."

"Very well then—"

Yes! She had succeeded. He would open the door and—

"—sit down," he instructed.

"What?"

"On the floor. Press your back to the door and listen."

Not success, but another point to the vexing list. What did he have in mind now?

Well, wasn't much else to do. He'd locked the door, and

most assuredly had locked the outer door in the hall as well. Wouldn't she appear the brazen to go running around to check on it?

He thinks he can hold out longer than she? Ha! He did not have virtue on his side.

On the other hand, he *didn't* have virtue on his side. And the possession of such had ceased to hold any importance as of late for Madeleine. And the fact that she did still possess her virtue gave Fouquet the upper hand.

Wait a minute.

Why hadn't she thought of this until now?

The very fact that she had a virtue to worry about *did* give Fouquet the means to blackmail her, whether he knew it or not. So why not dispose of that one little problem? And with a husband in hand, the disposal of said problem should prove little difficulty.

Such a ruse! But a marvelous notion, at that.

"Madeleine?"

Yes, indeed, perhaps this charade would prove quite beneficial to her. As long as she played up to her husband's greatest desire.

Recalling his command, Madeleine settled onto the floor, stretched her legs out before her, and pulled the robe over them. She pressed her back against the door and felt the same pressure as he most likely did the same. "Very well, I'm sitting alone in my room, my back to the door, my toes wiggling expectantly. Now what?"

"Tell me about the meal we just finished," he said. "Did you like it?"

"I did, but *you* practically inhaled your food. Must I now recount the flavors so you may know the pleasures of taste?"

"I tasted my food. I just wanted to hear how you taste. Please, indulge me."

Indulge, he said. When the only indulgence she wished had

just separated himself from her by a locked door. What was *his* ploy?

"Madeleine? Are you still there?"

"Very well," she said on a disappointed sigh. "Food, you say? The pork was tender and filling, the sauce was exquisite . . ."

"No, no, no. How did it make you *feel?*"

"Feel?" Madeleine glanced to the table and thought for a while. She'd devoured the delicious supper. As she had devoured most meals since leaving the court. Memories of cold and picked-over meals would never be completely lost. "It made me feel good. Special."

"How so?" The syrupy voice permeated their barrier on a beguiling wave.

"When I was a child my meals came to me after the duchess had finished with them. We were never allowed to eat with the court, only after. But nothing usually remained, save cold pickings. Mother would always let me have the duchess's plate, for the woman did not eat much. Though she did touch everything and tear it to pieces. It was rare when I'd receive a meal untouched, on a clean plate."

The scent of what now remained on her plate carried to her nose. Wild mushrooms, smoke-infused meat, the elusive traces of dry red wine. Not at all unappetizing. All that mattered was the child inside her knew it was *her* meal, and she could let it sit there for ages and not worry that anyone else should touch it. "I feel privileged when I have my own plate. Special, like I said."

"Interesting. I'm sorry for the things you were forced to endure as a child."

"You mustn't be. I had a far better upbringing than those who lived on the streets. It's not as if I am wanting for a home or clothing."

"But when your papa dies? Where will you go then? Your mother?"

No, she would go home to Pierre's estate in the Marais, one of the oldest and most elegant quarters in Paris.

Unless de Pellison changed her address.

"As I've said, mother is in Venice."

"Perhaps you'll marry quickly."

"Only for love, Armand."

Only for love. Her words echoed in his head. So did her earlier words about doing things for those that you cared for. Yes, his family had reaped the rewards of his betrayals against the innocent. But only because he loved them so.

"What of *your* meal?" she inquired through the door. "How did it make you feel?"

Armand drew one knee up and rested his arm on it. The back of the door held his head straight. He absently ruffed his thumb against the thick plush of his velvet breeches. "The roast was uneventful, for I have tasted finer, but the wine was an exquisite burgundy, Chassagne-Montrachet, from the Knights of Malta—1560, I'm sure."

"I didn't see that information on the label. How can you know things like that?"

"I spent some time with a connoisseur. She taught me many things about wine."

"She? I see. Was she your lover?"

Armand smiled at the implying tone in Madeleine's voice. Rich, satisfying memories filled his thoughts. "Yes, she was. Simone de Villenieau taught me the intricacies of wine, and I taught her the intricacies of pleasure." Until he'd tired of her and had left a month later with a healthy sum and the jewels from her neck, freely handed over and with best wishes to boot.

"Madeleine?"

"I want you to teach me, Armand. Before we part ways I want to learn everything you can teach me of the intricacies of pleasure."

"And what of your request earlier this evening, the one in

which you wished me to kiss you as if in love? Do you also request love of me?''

''That might have been a momentary lack of discretion.''

''I don't think so. You were sincere. What if I cannot give you what you desire, Madeleine?''

''You sound as though it is direly important you do please me.''

A pause. Please her? What woman did not deserve pleasure? Especially one who attracted with such effortless precision. Straight to his heart Madame Medusa's charms had gone, straight to his heart.

''I do rather enjoy pleasing you. Perhaps there are a few things I can teach you.'' And so much more, he thought. Like tonight. She was learning the power of restraint. As was he. He'd thought this ruse would separate them and keep his mind where it should be, on business. But he couldn't deny he enjoyed talking to her. Even through a door. Now, for a simple good-night kiss, and off to an eventless sleep.

''Close your eyes, Madame Medusa.''

''Whatever for?''

''I'm going to kiss you.''

''Oh.'' Uttered on a sigh. What her surprised moments did to Armand's self-control.

''Are they closed?''

''Completely.''

''Very well then.'' Armand closed his own eyes. The better to vividly imagine her ruby lips before him, slightly parted, soft and ready, with the ghost of hundred-year-old burgundy flavoring her sighs.

''You cannot see me near you, but I can smell your desire. A wisp of red-berried yew, carried in from your walk with my brother in the gardens this afternoon, paints a welcome sash around your person. My eyes are closed, too, so I cannot see your lips, full and red as blood, but sweet as candy. It is that first touch, when your wine-tainted sigh slips over my lips and into my mouth that preaches patience. Can you feel my kiss, Madeleine?''

"It is as a reward of wine to a parched woman's thirst. Longer,'' she said. "Make it last all night. And deep, so deep.''

The woman certainly was not afraid of requesting all that she wanted. Armand liked that about her. So much.

"As long as the stars twinkle in the sky.'' He glanced toward the window. The heavy draperies were pulled, and he sat in complete darkness, for the sun had set hours ago. "And if you cannot see the stars, than I shall have to kiss you until you can taste them in your thoughts.''

"Taste them?''

"Yes. Don't you suppose a star tastes much like your feeling special does? A satisfying glow that fills you completely, a taste and sensation you want never to end?''

"Like your kisses.''

He nodded and crossed his arms over his chest. "Exactly. I can taste the mushroom sauce from the roast on your tongue as I kiss you. It is sassy like you, but barely there, so much unlike you. Open your mouth wider, *chérie,* let me dive inside you. I want to partake of your flavor, your boldness, your sauciness.

"Mm, that lower lip. It's thicker than the top, I've noticed. A perfect dessert for my feast. I'm sucking it now, that plump, delicious morsel of star-dusted heaven. I can see the stars when I kiss you, Madeleine.''

He paused, for his fantasy was beginning to tingle on his lips. And other places. His hands were moist and his lower lip tender from him biting it. And his loins had begun to pulse, warning, expecting . . .

"Kiss my neck, Armand. I love it when you kiss me there. It does such marvelous things to me. Please?''

Memory of her wild antics in the carriage flushed Armand with the urge to relive that moment. "Mm, yes, that pale column of flesh, so tender that every touch of my lips causes you to react. And it affects different parts of your body. A kiss here, just below your ear . . .''

He heard a sigh. Definitely a sigh. A sweet reward to his own restraint.

''Your shoulders arc back, lifting your breasts high and into my reach. As I kiss you there, slowly running the tip of my tongue up to the point beneath your chin, you hike a leg up and squirm in my arms. I know you can feel my touch all over your body in exact twinges.''

''Like a harp string,'' she whispered. ''I feel that every one of your kisses plucks me and sets my entire being to a throb.''

''Yes, and just when you begin to waver more quickly and more closely you might suddenly lose that vibration . . . unless I kiss you again. Hard, and with my teeth, skating, running them along the side of your neck. Can you feel that, Madeleine? Have I plucked the right string?''

He could only imagine that she sat on the other side of the door writhing in desire. The steady stream of sighs that permeated the slab of wood set between them clued him that she might. She longed for his touch, his real touch. And right now, he could do with a bit of body contact himself.

Armand reached up and slid a finger over the crystal door pull.

No. That would be giving in. Armand Saint-Sylvestre never surrendered.

Instead, he quietly eased the lock from its metal fixing. Soundless. She would never know.

''Armand?''

''I'm still here. Still kissing your winter-pale flesh. That combination of creamy skin and red hair is so damned bewitching, you know that? And those cat's eyes.'' Flashes of her masked eyes that first night, defying him to follow her. And he had followed her. Right into this odd fantasy of seduction and defiance and very strange foreplay.

''Don't stop kissing me,'' she gasped. ''Continue, or I shall have to run into the hallway and pound on the outer door, waking all who stay at Vaux. If you refuse to let me into your chambers, you must at least grant me that."

"And if I did refuse," he mused. "If I barred both doors and ceased communication for the night, what would you do? Would you close your eyes and snuggle into bed, falling easily to sleep?"

"I'd not sleep to know you lie so close, and to feel the promised kisses you granted lingering in the air between us like a leprechaun's pot that must be claimed."

"You've already laid a claim on me, Madame."

"But you'll not allow me to enjoy the spoils of victory."

"Perhaps another kiss. But . . . lower?"

"Yes."

"Place your hands over your breasts, Madeleine. Tell me what you feel."

Silence told him she hesitated. But a tiny moan crept under the narrow slit below the door and tuned his own strings to a taut hum.

"Heavy and hot and hard," she listed for him. "My body is desperate for more than imaginary kisses."

"What are you wearing beneath that frustratingly modest robe?" His interest grew more acute with each and every gasp, each slip of fabric across marble floor or supple flesh.

"My chemise. It's dreadful thin, for I've had it for years. Oh, but I don't think I can feel your touch through this fabric, it's just so . . . impenetrable."

Before he knew what he was doing the cool circumference of the doorknob turned under Armand's palm. The door swung inside his room. He caught Madeleine's shoulders and lowered her to the floor. The faint glow from the candle sitting upon the armoire illuminated her body. Her eyes were closed, her lips pursed. Her hands, initially cupped over her breasts, reached for him.

After ripping the fragile ties at her neck, Armand slipped

his hand inside her chemise, the long opening cut to the center of her stomach, and found a wanting handful of hot flesh. She gripped his head, forcing him down to her breast.

But a wanting man can never truly be forced.

A hard bead of nubby flesh slipped under and around his tongue as he greedily fed from her exquisite plate of desserts. Two selections were offered this evening, and he intended to devour them both. Madeleine's moans and whimpers and grasping fingers only served as a delicious crème sauce poured over the entire feast.

"Once again, I am victorious," she declared as she drew her fingers up under his doublet. "But I do so enjoy how my prey desires to please me."

"You claim victory too soon, my confident one."

Armand sprang back from his attack, raked both hands through his hair, moist with perspiration, and then stood. Indeed, she had been victorious. Again, damn it! Where had all his self-control gone? And why did he allow himself even to desire this woman?

"Time to retire, the lessons in pleasure are finished for this evening." He reached out and helped her up.

Pouty lips drew his attention, but the sight of her breast springing out of the thin chemise was almost more than he could bare. Almost. Armand crossed his hands behind his hips and pressed his back to the wall near the door. "Good eve, Madame."

Madeleine tossed her head back and gave a chuckle, a deep throaty chuckle that boasted of pleasures she'd not yet had. Her mane of fiery curls had been mussed and now flared all about her shoulders.

If Armand looked too long her snakes would triumph.

"You've gone and done it again, leaving me at some high peak of desire and want. Makes me wonder what condition you are in."

"Me?"

"Yes." She pressed up against him, and before Armand could move her hand rested over his breeches. "As I thought." She squeezed, and he jerked his head against the wall to stifle a moan. "Will it stay like this all night?"

He grabbed her wrist, but she had started to ease her palm up and down, which pulled his soft wool underbreeches back and forth over his rod. A sensation too remarkable to stop. "It will not," he forced out.

"How long?"

"If you remain it will be much sooner than if you do not."

"Really?"

"Madeleine, please." This time he did stop her motions; instead he laid his palm over her hand right where it was. The pressure, the heat of her contact, made him see light even behind his closed lids and in the darkness of his room. "You are advancing into a part of the game of which you know nothing."

"Teach me," she whispered strongly in his ear. The tip of her tongue flicked his lobe. Sweet heaven, was that a snake's tongue, or an angel's kiss?

"In good time," he enunciated carefully, and pulled her hand away. "All rewards come to those with the patience to wait."

In a swift motion, he pushed her over the threshold, closed his door, and locked it. Complete darkness sweatered the room. Madeleine's burst of frustration punctuated her slap against the door. And then all was silent.

He had won this one.

The pulsing muscle in his breeches protested, *But was it worth it?*

Nine

Now where could a wayward spy have gotten himself off to on a fine Sunday morning? Madeleine checked the door that separated their bedchambers. Unlocked, but Armand was not inside. Most vexing.

So she finished her breakfast of smoked salmon and wine and left Armand's portion on a silver tray at the head of his bed, figuring he was probably out spying somewhere. In which case, she had better find him. Fouquet would expect another report. But she had nothing more to relay beyond the fact that Armand was an excellent kisser and a master seducer.

But what had gotten into his head last night to separate the two of them? Had Armand's desire to debauch her grown cold? Or had the introduction of a wooden barrier been his own brand of seduction? Not that the barrier had worked all that long. It had been he that had finally surrendered.

She had won that round. According to Madeleine's tally that made two for her and zero for Armand.

She wondered now if he'd ever make a move to score his

own point. There was something holding him back from a full-
out passionate assault on her person. What it was, she did not
know.

If she would have allowed him to make love to her on their
wedding night, she wouldn't be worrying about this right now.
For then the threat Fouquet thought he held over her would be
useless.

Ah, she could not wait to return to Paris, if only for a change
of clothing. Three days in a row in the same dress wasn't so
unusual, but when she was trying to entice a man to fall in
love with her a change of scenery might prove fortuitous.

Madeleine studied her reflection in the gilded mirror hung
in the pink-and-yellow-striped tiring room, recalling Armand's
compliment last night. He'd said her hair and skin proved a
bewitching combination. If he only knew what that meant to
her!

But a close study of her face now proved her freckles were
starting to show through the light dusting of powder. She had
used the last of her Lady de Winter's face cream yesterday.
When her face was completely clean those damned freckles
mapped copper splotches all over. Hideous. And when she was
embarrassed, or blushed, they brightened all the more. Far from
bewitching. She could not go another day without her disguise.

As she used her finger to scrape out the final streaks of face
cream from the glass pot, and then smooth it over the apples
of her cheeks, Madeleine wondered where to begin her search
for Armand. He could be almost anywhere. Though he had
seemed very curious about the structures going up behind the
château. Alexandre had explained that was where the silver fir
stage was being erected for the fête.

Madeleine wondered what play would be performed, and
for a moment felt a twinge of regret at not being one of the
performers.

Though she had only flirted with acting for a month after
Pierre's death, that had been time enough to discover the hidden

mystery that had lain dormant inside her. When on stage the whole world loved her. A tangible feeling of freedom overwhelmed with each trip before the footlights. Her soul soared. A feeling very similar to being held in Armand's arms. The passion and desire he stirred in her weaved through her veins and meshed tightly in her heart. Never had she felt so important than when in Armand's eyes.

Though she knew he hadn't wanted this marriage, his touches, his looks, made her feel as though *he* had chosen *her* out of that crowd at Versailles.

"As much as I despise being blackmailed, I've one thing to thank Fouquet for," Madeleine said with a fluff to her hair in the mirror. "Armand Saint-Sylvestre."

She hooked her fingers through the eyeholes of her mask and sailed down the hallway, the thought to concern herself with obtaining incriminating evidence quite absent from her mind.

The back of the château extended to a vast patio of bleached stone, bordered by marble vases and statuary so pristine even the birds hadn't the heart to splatter them with their droppings. Everywhere workers hoisted wood planks and pounded nails and stroked thick paintbrushes over finished sections of what would prove to be a grand stage. Groundsmen raked up the crushed stone as quickly as the building supplies were lifted into place. Here and there horses strained against taut leather reins to heft their heavy loads.

Madeleine reached back to tie the velvet mask around her head, but she startled at the touch of fingers to her own. With Armand's name on her tongue she spun round.

"It has been a long time, M-Madame."

She knew that stuttering voice. Madeleine thought she'd seen the last of this lech months ago after she'd told him point-blank never to touch her again, or to even dream of touching. "Monsieur Molière, I should have guessed you would be the one behind such an elaborate stage. Entertaining the king?"

"In but a few days' time. Ah, b-but M-madame de Pellison you look ra-r-ravishing as ever." He reached to touch her hair but she jerked away, and he retreated as if flames had singed his fingers. "Oh, come, you are not still p-p-playing the tease?"

"Tease? I'll have you know that acting is not considered teasing."

"But the way you used to say your lines, and look at m-me," he waxed with both hands pressed to his stained shirt. "C-come, love, you must admit you are as thrilled as I to be at Vaux at the same time. Which room is y-yours, darling? I could stop by l-later with a part in the play. You'd be performing for the king."

She slapped at his pining hands. "I shall expect my husband will be most infuriated to learn you cannot keep your hands from my person."

"H-hus-b-b-b-band? But he's dead."

"I've married again." Pleased that her announcement chilled her opponent to the meek little worm that he was, Madeleine propped her hands on her hips, and declared, "We are honeymooning here at Vaux. He's a most important military man. At this very moment he's involved in a secret mission."

"Military, eh?" Molière doffed the brim of his hat, bringing it lower to shade his eyes and his chagrin. "I suppose c-con-con—best wishes are due. Indeed. Very well, then, I should be seeing to the con-con-con—building now. Good day, Madame."

Thinking not to let him off so easily, an impish streak prompted Madeleine to ask, "Might I still have that part you mentioned?"

"P-pa-p-part?"

"I thought as much." Spinning on her heels, Madeleine marched away.

That had been easy enough. She rather thrilled at seeing Molière shot down. Not that he was unkind, it was just those damned hands of his had minds of their own. There was only one pair of hands that she desired to touch her, and she would locate them soon enough.

"Alexandre, I've the most shocking news!"

Alexandre straightened over the open circle of box shrubs that formed the end of a curl deep within the left parterre on Vaux's front lawn. He pressed a hand to the base of his spine to ease out the crick produced by bending for hours.

Shocking news? Coming from Sophie's lips that could only mean she'd worn the incorrect color to salon, for wasn't Pomegranate Leaf in style last season?

"Where are the children?" he asked, as she sallied between the tight curves of hedging. "Does Marie have them under wing?"

"They're napping," Sophie said with a dismissive sigh. Always her sighs registered as gray puffs before Alexandre's eyes. Distasteful and ugly.

She gripped Alexandre's arm, and he could feel she was ready to fall. Exertion beyond a walk from the nursery to her bedchamber or a brisk descent from the front steps wasn't in Sophie's regular itinerary.

"You shouldn't submit yourself to such stress, Sophie. Here, sit down." He helped her to a nearby stone bench and when he wanted to stand, her grip held him down by her side. Foreseeing a discussion, Alexandre winced. He'd much rather be tending the gardens than speaking to his wife.

"What is it that's got you out of temper? Stop huffing, Sophie, you'll faint like you always do. If you wouldn't tighten your stays so."

"You speak as if you would know just how tight they are," she snapped. "When was the last time you bothered to loosen them, hmm?"

Always, she demanded such attention! Sit with me, Alexandre. Kiss me, Alexandre. Please, can't we make love tonight,

Alexandre? The woman was entirely too needy. She would never understand that his work was more important to him than anything. Save the well-being of his daughters.

"I'm sure you didn't come running across the grounds just to demand I loosen your stays."

"The effort would very well kill me if I should." Plumping her curls with a fist, she then spread her arms wide to make a grand announcement. "I've just come from speaking to Monsieur Molière."

"Ah, what a lark, have you decided to try your hand at acting? I should think you'd fare very well on stage."

"Horrors." She fanned her heaving bosom with a pudgy hand and blew repeatedly upward, which set the row of tight blond coils to a rhythmic swing. "You would approve of your wife acting upon the stage?"

"I think it would be splendid. It would give you something to do when you're not chasing after the girls. Expand your horizons beyond—" He stopped before saying, *your daily toilette.*

"My father would turn over in his grave were I ever to take to the stage. It's frightful enough that he died loathing me for marrying below my station."

Yes, yes, not a day must go by without Sophie twisting that important little detail into his skull. But had it been *his* fault she'd gotten pregnant? Well, perhaps so. Though, not entirely his. Sophie could be blamed for initially luring him into her arms with her dulcet giggle and a hot kiss to his ear. He'd thought her a brazen that night at the tavern years ago, not a socialite. How things had changed!

"Molière had a rather interesting tidbit of information regarding Armand and his red-haired coquette."

"Don't call her that. Madeleine seems a very pleasant woman. What could Molière possibly know about my brother and his traveling mate?"

"This one will shock even you."

* * *

The need to talk to someone about Fouquet's comings and goings pressed Armand to seek out his brother. The afternoon sun was most unbearable, lending to the lack of shade trees on the grounds, and was most likely the culprit in chasing the workers toward the stables for a refreshing siesta under the shade of a fringed tent. Though Armand was surprised not to find his brother in the thick of labor; the man was a workhorse. Pleasure was not a word in his vocabulary.

Of course, any man whose dictionary contained *Sophie* could certainly not be allowed the entry *pleasure.*

Savoring a wry grin at his musings, Armand stepped from the wide lawn walk. His boots crunched across the stone border that surrounded the twin parterres.

"Armand!"

Alexandre's head popped up from behind a conical shrub. He waved Armand over with a garden implement that caught the sun and flashed a beam of buttered silver.

"I had given up on finding you," Armand said as he grasped the wooden bucket his brother thrust out and held it stomach level. Alexandre carefully pruned the shrub with iron scissors, each branch tip being deposited into the bucket so as not to muss the grounds. "I should have known better than to expect you'd be taking a break."

"You know me well, brother." Alexandre straightened and pushed the back of his hand across his perspiring brow. "A hell of a lot better than I know you."

His accusing tone was the most unnatural thing Armand had ever placed on his brother. Alexandre was always so impartial as to cause great arguments between the Saint-Sylvestre siblings. The man simply would not take sides.

Slipping the pruning shears in a leather ring riveted to the belt around his waist, Alexandre hooked both hands at his hips and looked to the sky. "She's beautiful, your . . . partner."

"Madeleine?" Armand shrugged. "Indeed."

"That musical hair, those dulcet eyes alight with mysteries yet to be discovered."

Armand smiled at his brother's description of Madeleine. He was a man who saw the world in a unique way. Colors held musical qualities, voices took on shape. There were times Armand wondered what it would be like to spend a day in his brother's body, exploring the world in such a distinct and whimsical way.

"I can see that it was easy enough for a woman of her beauty to capture such a notorious pretender," Alexandre remarked.

"A thief no more. And I wouldn't say she's got as firm a hold on me as you might like to think, brother."

"Really."

It vexed Armand, this chilled mood his brother took with him. "Out with it, man. Something troubles you, I know it."

"Sophie just came to me with some rather interesting news. Gossip, perhaps, knowing Sophie. But I have a feeling this bit of gossip might have some truth in it."

Highly unlikely. Armand also knew Sophie; they'd shared the Saint-Sylvestre cottage for a year and a half before Alexandre had been commissioned to work with Le Nôtre.

Armand crossed his arms over his chest and kicked a heel out before him. "Go on, enlighten me about your wife's wise words."

"It seems Molière told Sophie he'd had the pleasure of meeting her sister-in-law earlier today."

A swallow caught in Armand's throat at the accusing tilt of Alexandre's head.

"Madeleine told Molière she was your wife. And while domestic chains are about the last thing I expect to find wrapped around your neck, I wonder if it really is true? I don't think there's a man a hundred leagues from here who could resist an evening spent wrapped in the curls of her hair."

Armand heeled the ground, twisting, until he noticed the

tension in his brother's expression at the sight of his desecrating the finely manicured lawn.

Hell! He could not lie to Alexandre, there was no sense in it. To betray his family would only make his journey to a clean beginning all the more difficult. In fact, he would have never lied in the first place had he not been sure this marriage would be ended, and it would not matter anymore.

"It's a long story, rather a lark, the whole thing."

"I've time."

"It's only temporary."

"So it's true?"

"We married a few days ago. I was drunk. Well, no, I'd been drinking. I regained my senses as soon as her father caught me with my hands up her skirt."

Now that he spoke of it, Armand had to wonder how Papa fared? Perhaps he should send for word from Les Invalides? Should coffin measurements be taken?

"So you do not love her?"

"Most certainly not. Well . . ." No. Of course not! Though he did favor Madeleine. Damn his libido, it certainly had a mind of its own. "It's merely a matter of a bargain having been struck."

"A bargain? What the hell is going on, Armand? Is this another of your ploys? *Mon dieu,* man, have you already given up on the guards and succumbed to your former ways?"

"No, no, never!"

Angered that his brother could even think such a thing, Armand paced past him and zoned his vision out on the line of pruned lime trees that closed the expansive property in on two sides. How it wrenched his heart even to think his family could not trust him. Though Alexandre had never condoned his taking to the high roads to support the family, he'd never condemned Armand either, and had grudgingly accepted money to purchase his botany books.

"Forgive me, but I do not know what to think, brother. I

know you too well. You will die a bachelor to escape the chains of marriage you believe shackle all men.''

''As I've seen you shackled.'' Armand turned and just caught the agreeing nod of his brother's head. As much as he tried to show some compassion toward Sophie, Alexandre was not a man who could hide his feelings with a pleasant expression or remark. ''Don't worry, Alexandre, this is only for a short while. I—she . . . well, there's a bit more to the story.''

Alexandre quirked a brow. He knew too well the wiles of a female desperate to marry.

''I have garnered a mission from Colbert in order to prove my loyalty to the crown and gain a commission in the guards. The household troops is where I belong.''

''Indeed. And the increase in pay will no doubt serve the expensive taste you have come to desire over the years.''

''Hardly.'' But now was no time to explain his real need for increased wages. ''Anyway, I've been assigned to follow Fouquet. There was a fête at Versailles the other night. I had relaxed my guard for a moment . . . Madeleine danced into my arms and kissed me. Half an hour later I married her.''

No words were needed to interpret Alexandre's openmouthed gape.

''You know what a beautiful woman does to me.''

''Your one weakness. But I thought it a weakness you had conquered for the sake of honor.''

''I was soused. I craved a night with a nameless woman. It had been a while since I'd bedded a woman.''

''Hard to believe.''

Yes, yes, his days of womanizing were indeed blissful murals painted at the back of his mind. But memories only.

''There was something in her eyes. Damn it!'' He speared the air with a fist. ''I should not have looked in her eyes! Desperation pleaded in those sky-colored eyes. As you've said, they were alight with mystery.''

Alexandre crossed himself. "Thank goodness for Sophie's soundless flat eyes."

"Suffice it to say, both Madeleine and I have agreed to an annulment. She was only going along with her father's dying wish."

"Have you made love to her?"

"Not yet—"

"Don't."

Armand glanced at his brother's gesture, his long fingers tersely slicing the air.

"Unless you wish to be trapped."

Enough said.

"I am trying not to," Armand said. "But it isn't the easiest task when one must sleep in the next room as the Medusa-haired Madeleine. Damn, she is playing with my mind. Every coy whisper, every bat of her lash, loosens my resolve. It's almost as if she is the seducer and I the seduced."

"Finally, a woman who would challenge the master himself, eh?"

"But she has come into my life at the wrong time. I must remain impartial to her wiles. My mission will fail if I do not concentrate."

"Mission?" Alexandre thumbed a trimmed tip of the nearby yew. "And I'd thought it was merely family that brought you to Vaux."

"You know I would visit every day if I could. If you didn't have to live so damned far away. Colbert has hired me to spy on Fouquet. The king suspects the financier of dipping into the royal coffers. I'm to report back anything I find."

"Um ..." Alexandre's eyes widened, and he stabbed his shears at something located just over Armand's right shoulder. "Madeleine!"

Hell. Armand swung around to find his wife standing next to a column of yew. She slipped the velvet mask from her face. "Madeleine. Er, um ... what did you hear?"

She shrugged and sauntered over to him, twirling the mask near her hip. Drawing a delicate finger under his chin and casting a triumphant glimmer from her bewitching eyes, she said, "Enough to know this is not a pleasure visit."

Ten

Success.

The letter Madeleine now held would soon be en route to the Louvre with the name of Armand's employer scrawled for Fouquet's eyes. It had been fortunate to stumble upon Armand and his brother at the moment they had been discussing his mission.

Jean-Baptiste Colbert, eh? So that was the man who suspected Fouquet of stealing. The two court advisors were notorious rivals. Madeleine was surprised Fouquet had not guessed his shadow. Ah, well, it did not concern her, beyond the fact that she now had the exact information Fouquet had requested of her.

She handed the missive to the lackey Fouquet had sent along, but a *whoosh* of air rippled the paper and tore it from her hand.

"Armand!"

He displayed his sword, the letter dangling from the tip. "What have we here?"

He almost had it in his grasp—but Madeleine was quicker.

"Not that it is any of your concern, but this is a letter for my cousin who lives in the Marais." She pressed it into the lackey's hands and had to move quickly between the boy and Armand. "Why the sudden concern over my correspondence?"

"I wasn't aware you had reason to write anyone, Madame. Who is this cousin? You've made no mention of her."

"Her name is Valérie Découvertes." She turned to the lackey. "Now go, deliver the missive to the address I gave you." The Louvre. Not the Marais. But Armand must not know.

"Pray she can read around the sword cuts," she shot at Armand. But he did not receive her demeaning glare, for he now stood with his back against the wall, his eyes closed.

So he felt horrible for what he had done. Good. That had been a close one. Had he been more curious, her cover might have been destroyed.

She opened the door to her room, but Armand did not follow, so she closed it behind her and strode purposely away from danger.

Madeleine breathed a wistful sigh and settled before the vanity near the window that overlooked the front gardens. Curiously, Armand remained in the hall. Did he follow the lackey? Pray not. She would have heard his heels echo down the marble hall. Perhaps he was still collecting his resolve, preparing an apology for his rude actions before coming inside the room.

Indeed, she had played that one well.

Madeleine tipped the end of her sable brush, thick as her fist, over the powder tin then dusted her décolletage. She leaned forward, scrutinizing her cheeks. Nervous and feeling as if she'd just outrun a cougar, she noticed her fright suffused her face with heat. "I need more of Lady de Winter's cream. I shouldn't wish Armand to see the horrid spots beneath."

A puff of fine lilac-scented powder took to air as she set the brush on its pewter holder. Twisting her hair into a chignon, Madeleine held it against the back of her head while she vacillated between wearing her hair up or finding a maid to plait it.

"I prefer it down."

Madeleine startled at the deep, whispery voice and dropped the coil of her hair. Curly tresses splayed out across her shoulders, but were taken up by Armand's hands. She hadn't even heard the door open. Had the cougar returned to toy with her?

Armand plunged his nose into a thick clutch of her hair as if it were a bouquet of fragrant roses. From over her shoulder, he looked at her surprised reflection. "Wear it down."

She couldn't gauge from his expression whether or not he had believed her excuse about writing to her cousin. Reaching for her brush, Madeleine began to pull it through her hair. A distraction would be required to keep the man's thoughts from their encounter in the hall.

"Forgive my rudeness. Perhaps it was a moment of jealousy, seeing you standing there with that man, handing him a secret missive." He tilted his head and studied her fingers lazily weaving the brush through her hair.

"Man? He was but a boy." Madeleine paused as she felt his reflected gaze heat through her flesh and course a fiery path across her exposed shoulders and down to her breasts. So he had been more jealous than curious!

"You see how you've got me at odds? I find challenge in every man's close proximity to my beautiful wife."

How his words claimed her. The scent of Armand's fire lingered about her shoulders like a cloak of storm-brewed mist. Seduced by her desires, Madeleine replayed his voice over in her thoughts. *My beautiful wife, my beautiful wife . . .* So very different from the taunts of her childhood.

No! He could not speak the truth. *This man is trouble, his past only proves it,* she thought. *Keep on your toes.* The game must be played until she received word that Fouquet was satisfied.

"All is forgiven." She scanned the vanity, seeking a diversion. "I'm out of powder." She added a pout for effect. "Now I shall never hide these dreadful freckles."

"Freckles?"

"They are hideous."

"I don't see anything. Come here."

For a reluctant moment, Madeleine just stared at his gesturing fingers. It was as though Armand held command of all he encountered and might never expect that anyone should refuse him a thing. His tempting nod returned Madeleine to her struggles against wanting him and needing just to walk away from the man she betrayed every single moment she remained in his presence.

Ah, but she mustn't let him suspect she was troubled by anything other than common womanly complaints such as cosmetics and gowns. She stood and allowed him to place his hands upon her hips.

For a moment he merely held her like that, assurance a proud vestment he wore with ease. Then he ran the back of his finger down the side of her face, inwardly pleased when she dipped her head to meet his touch. He held his fingertip before her so she could see the smudge of white powder he'd wiped away. Horrors! Madeleine thrust her hand up to cover her exposed freckles, but he caught her wrist.

"They are not dreadful. I rather like them. Not that I can see them without getting nose to nose with you."

She brightened, lowering her hand. "Really?"

Armand nodded. "You've the loveliest skin ever."

Madeleine blushed at his effortless comment. Many men had gifted her with compliments over the years: actors, musicians, powdered and mouched court fops. But this man possessed one thing all others could never hope to obtain. An effortless power of seduction. *Savoir faire.*

She observed as Armand picked over her pots and dishes and brushes arranged on the vanity.

"What do you need all these accoutrements for anyway?"

What *did* she need them for? To look fashionable. If her skin were not corpse white and her lips crimson, then she would be shamed at court. Not that she would put in an appearance at court unless it was onstage. Truly she did not need these accoutrements, as Armand had put it. Save the face cream that would cover her freckles. That was her safety screen. For to reveal herself totally to a man—to anyone—well, Madeleine shuddered to even think of it.

"I don't use much more than my dusting powder and my Lady de Winter cream. But"—she sighed—"I've run out. Oh, it's perfectly dreadful. It's de Winter's cream that masks my freckles."

"I should wish to see them from this day forth."

But she wasn't ready to give up her safety shield just like that! "Oh, but it also keeps my skin soft and . . . touchable."

She cradled Armand's hand, directing his exploratory fingers over her jaw, until he journeyed unguided down her neck.

"Very touchable," he said, lost in his travels. He kissed her and just when Madeleine had stepped over the edge again, he pulled away, seeming to surface groggily from a dream, and blink his eyes to bring himself back to reality.

"Is something amiss?"

"Indeed." He dashed to the bed to retrieve his sword. "I've work to do. Now that you know who I work for and what I am doing—"

She rushed after him. "Why would you say that?"

"Come, Madeleine, you don't think I believe you did not hear my conversation with Alexandre earlier?"

"I didn't."

"Madeleine."

"Well, maybe a little."

"Maybe all?"

His gaze, penetrating and powerful, stole away Madeleine's willpower. "Maybe a bit more than a little . . . oh . . . very well, I heard every word. Yes, I know about Colbert. But what does it matter?"

"It matters immensely should that information fall into the

wrong hands. You must promise me your utmost discretion, Madeleine. My success relies on secrecy. No one can know what I am at Vaux for. If Fouquet were ever to find out—''

"I promise," she blurted out.

"Good. Now." He smoothed his hands over her shoulders, and pressed his cheek to hers, finding her in the mirror with those passionate, all-knowing eyes of his. "Tell me I can trust you, Madeleine."

"Trust? Er, oh"—she glanced away, drew her eyes up the door behind them—"but of course you can." She could not meet his eyes—knew she should—but could not bear to see the reflection of her dishonesty.

"You would not betray me?"

"Huh? Oh . . . no. Never." Blood pounded in her ears. This was terribly cruel. She did not want to lie to this man. Not anymore.

He placed his hat on his head, the white plume dusting his shoulder, and snapped the brim. "I hope you will not, Madame. Now, I'm off for a moment, then I shall return for you. I don't wish to remain at Vaux any longer than necessary. Perhaps you might spend the afternoon in the sun with Sophie and the children?"

She cast him a narrow glance.

"Perhaps not. But I'm sure Alexandre would enjoy your company. He, er . . . he knows we are married. We had just been discussing that before you surprised us in the gardens. Sophie told him."

Too shocked to speak, Madeleine was still stuck on the promise she had made not to betray his confidence.

"Gossip travels fast," he said, opening the door to leave. "You should watch whom you tell your many secrets to, Madeleine."

"But I didn't—"

"I believe the information came from Monsieur Molière? Well, I'm off."

He closed the door. Molière?

Oh yes, she'd told him she was married to fend off his advances.

What a spy she was!

And what a horrid, horrid liar she had become. To betray Armand so cruelly had suddenly become the worst of all sins. It was time to stop. She didn't want to hurt Armand anymore with her duplicity.

But how to extricate herself from Fouquet's grasp without losing a fortune in the process?

The final of a half dozen silver letter openers sailed through the air and found its place in the thick oak door next to its mates. Nicolas Fouquet fanned the shredded missive before his face for the sixth time, severing words and letters with a curt slice. He'd received word from Madeleine this morning naming Colbert as Saint-Sylvestre's employer.

Fouquet wrenched the heavy sausage-curled wig from his head and tossed it to the floor in a black heap. He pressed both palms to his head, twisted against the sweaty strands of itchy hair that took refuge all too often beneath a wig, and squeezed.

To learn his greatest enemy had successfully planted a spy in his home! He should have suspected as much that first day he'd noticed Saint-Sylvestre lingering in the shadows of the Louvre. Valérie's maid had been in for a request for funds that day, and had been startled to recognize the man after Fouquet had pointed him out to her. The very man who had seduced her mistress months earlier.

An interesting announcement. With some careful sleuthing, Fouquet had discovered much about Saint-Sylvestre's past. But not enough about his present.

And now to discover it was Colbert whom Saint-Sylvestre worked for!

And he with his ridiculous excuse for a spy following the bastard around.

Rattling his finely pointed little fingernail against the side of his desk, Fouquet stewed for a moment, before ripping the slender shreds of Madeleine's handwriting before his face. "De Pellison!"

No answer. Fouquet scrambled through his desk drawer, seeking a weapon, a projectile, anything. He produced a sharpened quill. But the feather pen did not sail toward the target as well as the letter openers.

"De Pellison! Damn that man, where is he?"

Fouquet pushed away from his desk and bent forward, catching his forehead in his hands. "Colbert will not rest until he sees me fall!"

"So Madame Medusa is in need of face cream to cover her freckles, eh?"

From what he'd seen, he rather liked the sweet little marks sprinkled across her nose. Why did women insist on creating masks of their countenances when beneath lay the real treasure?

Ah, it was society, Armand knew that well enough. He'd not spent a fortune on wigs and silver-tipped scabbards a few years back just for his health. Society demanded men and women appear a certain way in public if they wished acceptance by the *beau monde*. A man must have a curled wig; women, pale, flawless skin. A man should wear slashes in his doublet and lace at his wrist, a woman should cinch her waist to half its circumference and shuffle her bodice as low as possible for maximum exposure of her treasures.

Touching the lace that circled his wrist, Armand smirked. All right, then, so he had no dispute with fashion. It certainly made the female figure delightful to behold. He could appreciate a smooth, pale cheek as well as the next man as long as he never forgot that beneath the masks and frippery lay a person as false as his or her exterior.

Armand frowned as he rummaged through a stack of plans for the elaborate stage that was at this very moment being finished behind the château. He knew as much because he now held a detailed drawing of the finished product in his hands. Silver fir wood had been shipped from Holland for its creation. Price: forty thousand livres.

Pleased with his find, Armand placed the paper with the price in a separate pile from the design plans and lifted the lid on yet a third chest that he'd found cached behind a secret wall in Fouquet's study.

But his thoughts continued to stray.

He couldn't help but recall the missive Madeleine had skirted out of his command in the hallway. And to hear the name of the addressee. He'd been literally punched by an invisible blow to the gut, delivered by Madeleine's careless mention of her cousin.

Valérie Déscouvertes.

That name! To hear it spoken by Madeleine, without a clue as to what it meant to him!

Unless, she *did* know what Valérie meant to him.

How ironic that he should fall at the hands of the one woman he might have really had feelings for. The one woman he hadn't the courage to rob, or the heart to victimize.

Had he loved Valérie? Perhaps.

No.

If Valérie Déscouvertes were involved with securing Madeleine's presence in his life in any way . . .

Well, he could entirely expect that the woman might seek revenge against him. But in such a manner?

Ah! Armand had to leave Vaux immediately. He'd already compromised his cover by revealing himself to his brother and, inadvertently, to his wife! Indeed, he might have been wiser to follow Captain Lambert's plea to leave Madeleine in Paris.

He mustn't allow his craving for another touch, another kiss, to become an addiction.

Turning back to the box, Armand thumbed through a stack of papers. Columns of carefully scribed numbers flashed before his eyes. He placed the paper on the floor and bent over it. A crack of bright sunlight slipped through the wall and the secret door, enough so he could read.

The year 1661 dashed across the upper right corner of the document; three columns of numbers, and one column of words, filled the page. But instead of financial terms, the first contained odd references to honey. And crossroads? Also gates, speed, and nightshade. Very unusual. But someone had taken the time to write so carefully, and each number as exact as its match found elsewhere on the page.

He paged forward, finding there were six papers in all that contained such neat columns, and more odd words that couldn't possibly be classified in any group or division. Could these documents be coded?

What if he secreted these papers to Colbert, only to find they were useless, mere daily recordings of insignificant accountings? On the other hand, what if he left them as he had found them, perhaps the evidence of embezzlement Colbert sought?

Armand deliberated.

Captain Lambert's voice remarked, *"If you prove your loyalty to the king, a position in the guards is yours."*

"I'm so proud of you, Armand," his sister had said, *"how you've turned your life around."*

Have you ever done something that you know might be wrong, but would benefit someone you cared for with all your heart?

Yes, and this mission, besides serving himself, was supposed to serve the one woman he had hurt the most. A woman he'd thought to never have contact with again. But was now, once again, strangely entangled in his life.

Had Madeleine's mention of Valérie been just that? An innocent slip? There was no reason why she could not be related to the woman, and yet, have not a clue as to Valérie's involvement with Armand.

He hoped.

Now was no time to second guess his intentions. If Valérie were involved, he would deal with that later.

Carefully folding the papers in half, Armand then slid them inside his shirt. A clatter in the outer hall alerted him. He stuffed the plans and diagrams inside the storage chest and pulled the false wall back to fit into its groove, closing himself inside the musty closet.

"Taking the air?"

Madeleine spun round at the man's voice but could not see anyone standing in the shadow of the château's west side. With the construction sounds littering the air she couldn't truly be sure she had heard a voice. Gripping her mask to her breast, she called, "Who's there?"

With a grace and studied allure that he was famous for, Nicolas Fouquet stepped out of the shadows, one lace-festooned hand propped at his hip, the other hand toying with the long strands of coal-dark hair that hung nearly to his elbows.

"Monsieur Fouquet." Madeleine curtsied, not sure why, but couldn't help the unbidden motion. Her throat grew dry at sight of the preening financier, her heartbeats faster. "I did not see you standing there. I was just admiring your home, it is so lovely. I had no idea you were even in residence, for I would have sought you out upon my arrival. What *are* you doing here?"

"Won't you come out of the sun?" He gestured toward a glass-paned door, and Madeleine stepped up behind him. "It's dreadful hot today. I've some lemon ices from Paris that are in desperate need of consumption. Come, do not deny me a few moments with a lovely lady such as yourself before I must leave once again for Paris."

He was much too charming for belief. ''I don't wish to keep you from business.''

''Nonsense. Come, come.''

Not wanting to do this, but finding she followed the elegant man as if curious to see what his next move might be, Madeleine entered a small stateroom furnished in dark woods and gold damask and sat before a desk by which he then stood. A portrait of Fouquet, hung with braided black satin behind the desk, mastered the room. A whisper of a smile graced the picture's lips, the hidden evil perfectly masked by a boylike disposition.

On the desk sat an ice tureen. Frost had formed on the outside. From the inside, Fouquet produced a small silver cup of the aforementioned lemon ice. A charming finger-length silver spoon was also offered.

It looked tempting. But a niggling ache in Madeleine's gut warned her. Could she even trust him anymore? Armand had said Fouquet had stolen. What?

''I have just eaten, Monsieur.''

''You women and your need to retain a slender shape,'' Fouquet said in his artificially pleasant voice.

''I don't understand why you are here. You must have received my post?''

''Yes.'' He stabbed at the ice crystals with the spoon, his pinkie extended delicately to display the hideous long fingernail used by the court elite for scratching on the king's chamber door. ''I commend your quick response regarding Monsieur Saint-Sylvestre's mission. Though you neglected to mention what sort of mission it was.''

''But I gave you Colbert's name. Is that not enough?''

He settled into the chair behind the desk and produced a slip of paper, which he began to tap against his chin. Young, vibrant eyes held her captivated. It was almost as if she were a dog waiting for a table scrap. Until Madeleine took a better look at the paper tapping his chin. It looked like the folded post Madeleine had addressed to Valérie.

"Where did you get that? That was a private missive to my cousin."

"She will read it, I promise. But I must be aware of all correspondence between you and my niece, especially if it concerns Monsieur Saint-Sylvestre."

"Why? I thought you did not want Valérie to know about him?"

"Exactly." He looked up from her prose and speared her with a look. "Yet, in this very letter you deemed to wax over this new man you've traveled to Vaux with."

"I did not name him."

"It matters not; my niece mustn't be bothered by your romantic prattle." He laid the letter by the bucket. A smirk of knowing lit in his eyes. "You love the man already, don't you?"

"I—well no."

"Not according to your letter."

"I said nothing of the sort in that letter!"

"Ah, but it is all in the tone, my lady. All in the sound of the spaces between the words. The sighs . . ." He gave a grand sigh and pressed a swoonful hand to his chest. "The unexpressed adoration."

"Monsieur Fouquet, please, I shall do as you have asked—"

"When? Between love letters and kisses? My home is not to be used as a *maison de rendezvous* by any street whore who will have it!"

"Please." Unnerved, she flexed her fingers and tried to appear calm. There was just something about this man that made it difficult to speak her mind. "It was a part of your request my seducing the man."

"Yes, it was." He tapped the contents of the ice bucket, then touched his fingers to his mouth. Ice dew glittered on his lips. "Have you discovered yet why Monsieur Colbert would send Saint-Sylvestre to Vaux?"

"No. I know little about Armand, and even less about his profession."

"Yet you have spent two days with him. Some spy you are."

"I—I'm no professional by any means. It was you that selected me. What do you expect?"

"A hell of a lot more than you've given."

"Then release me from your bidding." She stood, prepared to leave. "I have given you Colbert's name."

"Oh, not so quickly, Madeleine." He sprang up and stopped her, pressed his palm against her shoulder and curled his fingers into her flesh. His touch was a warning, not yet dangerous. "I need to know why Colbert has sent your husband here."

His presence made her uneasy. Sensing that sharp little fingernail begin to dig into her flesh, Madeleine lost grasp of her resolve and sputtered, "He is here because Colbert believes you have stolen!"

"What?"

A drop of condensation dribbled through the frost crystals on the ice bucket, clearing a shiny path to the polished desk. It was a similar example of how this man made her feel, as if ice were sliding down the back of her neck. "He hasn't told me much; that is all I know."

"Me. Stolen? Hmm . . ." He paced toward the windows, tapping a finger against his jaw, then suddenly he swung around. "It is lies, scandalous licentious lies!"

"Obviously not, if Colbert has gone so far as to send a spy to your home."

"Give me time to think!"

No, it was her turn to command the conversation now. "I cannot do this for you anymore, Monsieur Fouquet. I will not!"

"Why not?"

"I am betraying Armand's trust!"

The laughter that peeled from his lips added insult upon the humility Madeleine already felt. "Betrayal? Ha! You are enjoying every bit of this charade, don't deny it."

"Not in the least."

A smirk and a glittering eye. "That's not what I've seen."

"You've *seen* nothing."

"As you've done nothing?"

His cryptic words startled, but Madeleine would not allow him the victory of seeing her shaken. *He just guessed that I have something to hide about my wedding night. He cannot know the truth.* She must make love to Armand. Soon!

"If you wish me to retain some modicum of secrecy, I must leave now, Monsieur Fouquet. I am sure my husband is looking for me."

"But of course."

She stepped around the desk, was almost to the glass doors, when—

"One last thing before you go, Madeleine. I *know* you did not sleep with Pierre de Pellison on the night you were wed."

She spun round. How could he possibly? "You are grasping for answers when you could not possibly know!"

"Then why so eager to do my bidding unless you know it to be true?"

Why indeed? Oh, he did know. Horrors!

"You know that I speak the truth, and it shall go straight to my secretary's ear if you do not comply with my wishes. I believe the discovery that the marriage vows were not consummated should give de Pellison grounds to have your inheritance stripped from you."

Mon Dieu. Madeleine sank with a pouf of skirts into the chair, her lungs—nay, her very soul—deflating as quickly as the satin fabric. How could he possibly know?

"So what will it be?" He hiked a leg up on the desk; the crunch of lemon ice grinding between his teeth rippled angrily down Madeleine's spine.

There was no doubt about her reply, for she could not bare to suffer the loss of her finances. Not now. If things had been different, if Valérie were well . . .

"I will get you more information," she said with what little bravery she could muster.

This man held too much power in the knowledge of her crime. No, not a crime, just an unfortunate situation. He'd played her bluff and had won. She should not have been so compliant, so eager to make him see that she wanted to protect the story of her wedding night from de Pellison.

"Excellent. Now, I'm needed back in Paris. I've arranged to have a lackey escort the two of you to the city this evening. No need to have that spy digging around in my things." The man curled a finger through the condensation on the ice bucket and drew it across his lips. He granted Madeleine one of his infuriatingly pleasant smiles—a practiced smile that masked the evil beneath. "Your financial future depends on your ability to charm Saint-Sylvestre. Whatever he knows about me, I must know. You understand?"

Ice coursed through Madeleine's veins at the touch of Fouquet's hand to her cheek. But she held strong, not flinching, lest he think for one moment she might lack the courage to carry out her task.

"He is nothing but a common thief, Madeleine. And remember, if you wish a man to spill his deepest secrets"—he whispered against her ear—"you do know what to do, don't you, my unfortunate virgin?" He looked into the mirror, pursed his lips ruefully, and locked on to her reflected gaze.

Swallowing her pride in the name of a small child's fate, Madeleine nodded to Fouquet's reflection and forced controlled words over her lips. "Of course."

As the door closed behind her quick departure Fouquet's words revisited her frazzled thoughts.

My unfortunate virgin.

Did he not realize that his own blackmail scheme would be thwarted as soon as she slept with Armand?

On the other hand, when finally she did sleep with Armand, the betrayal would be carved too deeply. She might receive the passion she so desired, perhaps even blind trust and a few secrets, but could a man who had once done the very same thing she was now doing—pretending, in order to gain riches— really fall victim to her seductions and fall in love with her?

Love?

The word thrummed in her breast. Pure and true and steadfast love. Something she had always desired. Something Madeleine wished from Armand.

Something she could now never have.

He waited what seemed an hour—though it might have been no more than ten minutes—before Fouquet's footsteps finally exited the office and the click of his heels made haste down the outer hallway.

Armand pushed against the heavy wall that served entrance to the secret chamber behind the desk.

What he had just heard!

Madeleine—cruel, clever actress that she was—was working for Fouquet! He had been duped by a saucy smile and a tempting kiss. Fouquet had known all along that he was spying on him and had sent his own spy in to even the score.

And he didn't want to begin to think on the mention of Madeleine's husband. Her *husband?* She had been married before? Or perhaps she was still married? And Fouquet—he had addressed her so blatantly—my unfortunate virgin?

Ah! This information was too devastating to comprehend. What would Captain Lambert think when he discovered this? And Colbert? What a spy he'd proven to be. Not only had Armand allowed the enemy into his own camp; he had *married* her.

Eleven

Stepping out into Fouquet's study, Armand clutched the coded reports in his hands. He swung the study door wide and took one step into the hallway when the crack of a musket and the whiz of a musketball skimmed past his nose.

Stunned, Armand stood fixed in the doorway, listening for the retreat of heels. He heard nothing beyond the dry rasp of the papers he'd gathered settling around his boots.

He gripped his arm, just above the elbow. Crimson stained the nap of his velvet doublet. The musketball had ripped a serrated gash through his doublet, shirt, and flesh.

He must pursue the shooter, but he could not leave evidence lying around for anyone to find. Keeping an eye on the turn at the end of the marble hallway, Armand bent and scooped the papers into his hands. Even as he worked quickly, he knew the chase was a loss. The shooter was either long gone—or . . . he could still be waiting to finish the job.

Crushing the papers to his chest, Armand prowled carefully toward the end of the hall. He paused, listened, but heard no

breath beyond his own, nor did he hear heels clicking in retreat.
With a quick dart, he lunged forward, only to find the adjoining
hallway empty.

He relaxed his guard and pressed his free hand to the wall.
A splash of blood colored the floor by his toe. Then another.

Zut alors! What the hell was going on?

First, the introduction of Valérie Déscouvertes to the plot.
Second, Fouquet's spy—his wife. And now . . . someone had
just attempted to kill him.

And he'd thought this mission a way of quenching his thirst
for adventure, of rekindling the danger and intrigue he'd once
thrived on?

An attempt on his life was beyond the call of adventure.
Right now, Armand much preferred to be absconding from a
rich widow's bed than to be walking the halls of Vaux.

A pot of black tulips had been placed upon her vanity that
afternoon, perhaps courtesy of the flower beds near the stables.
Madeleine touched a convex petal, wistful in her memories.
Had it truly been her father who had given her a tulip plant
for her sixteenth birthday? Or had it merely been one of her
mother's many lovers, grasping at a chance to win the daughter's affections in a quest for Cecile's heart?

She could never be sure, for the card merely said, from an
admirer. And the fleeting glimpse she'd gotten of the man's
exit from her mother's home provided but a back view of a
wide-shouldered man in cape and petticoat breeches. Another
fop.

That she had never known true family was the only regret
Madeleine could conceive of. When Armand had questioned
her about her ideas on family, she had spoken the truth. Family
truly was an intangible feeling. And she craved it desperately.

A door slammed in the adjoining room, signaling Madeleine
that Armand had returned. She snapped a crisp stem and held

the tulip up to her ear. On second thought, the dark bloom would not look so good in her hair; nor did it have a favorable smell.

The slam of the door that joined their rooms startled her. The fragile bloom snapped in her fingers. Black petals skimming over her skirts, Madeleine spun to face Armand.

A furious stride carried him past her and into the tiring room. He reappeared holding her tapestry bag, which he flung on the bed.

"Pack," he commanded. "We are off."

"Armand." She followed his angry strides back into his own room. "What is wrong?"

When he jerked the doublet from his arms she saw the blood on his upper arm. "Oh! What happened?"

He dusted her curious fingers away with a sharp slice of his hand. "Do not touch me, woman."

Stunned at his callous treatment of her, Madeleine froze on the spot. Woman? Had he been injured in the brain as well as the arm? "Armand, I don't understand."

He pinned her with a harsh look. Madeleine swallowed.

"You, my lady"—he pressed a hand to the wall just over her shoulder, blocking her between the wall and his body—"are guilty of the gravest betrayal. Were I not a gentleman, I would bodily toss you from this room. As it is, my temper only increases, so I warn you do not—I repeat, do not!—test the waters, for I will resort to such action if provoked."

"Oh," Madeleine gasped, fighting the dry stretch in her throat. Grave betrayal? He couldn't know. Could he? "I suddenly don't feel so well."

"Really. Is it sickness . . . or guilt?"

"Guilt?"

"I know, Madeleine. I know everything!"

"You—you know?"

"The ploy is up." He countered her, face-to-face. But this time the close proximity made her tremble not out of desire, but fear. "My spying trapped me in the closet of Fouquet's study just now while he had an interesting conversation with you. Oh, yes," he countered, before she could find the words upon her tongue. "I must admit you drew me into the marriage with great ease. Quite a talent you have for leading a man to believe your supposed desperation. To think I actually believed you and Papa were for real! You have begun to green, Madame."

"What?" she gasped. Her bodice had begun to squeeze in a most horrifying twist. A queasy wave circled her head. She did feel as green as he said she looked.

"You were not prepared for such information, I see. Worry not, I'll have you out of my hands soon enough. We leave immediately for Paris, where I shall deliver you to my captain."

"Armand, please!" She tried to touch him, to press a gentle calming hand to his own, but he snapped away.

A dark rage had been pulled over his usual sweltering charm. It chilled Madeleine to the bone to stand alone in the room with him. But his sudden declaration wrenched out her own desperation. "Do you think I would be so cruel as to purposely engage myself in such deception? I had no choice!"

"No choice? Death you've no choice, Madame. Every other option in life is just that, an option. No one forced you to trick me. No one forced you to take vows of matrimony with a man you knew well in advance you were to deceive."

He turned and gripped her chin, forcing her gaze up into his. The welcome doors had been slammed shut; no longer did Madeleine feel she belonged in such a hateful pair of eyes. "Convince me that you did not enter into this bargain with Fouquet willing and ready."

"I despise Fouquet. You must believe me."

"After what I've seen of your spirit, Madame, your spark, your defiance, how can a man possibly force you into such acts of betrayal?"

She matched his tirade with a firm jaw. "It wasn't force—exactly."

"You see? So how then am I to understand his methods to entice you into such a position? Spying? Nearly ransoming your virtue? All to keep one harmless spy under surveillance?"

"My virtue and my spying are two entirely separate things. The passion I desire did not direct my actions." Most of the time.

"You wouldn't have used sex to cajole information out of me?"

Now he was being outrageous. "Have you been physically overwhelmed and forced to reveal anything to me?"

That statement stymied him. But for a moment. "But *anything*, Madame—there was that promise. Can you not say that wasn't the hook in your plot?"

"It was entirely unplanned."

"And what does your husband know of your amorous ways, Madame?"

"My—my husband?"

"Yes, your other husband that is. I did hear mention of a husband."

"Then you must also have heard he is dead!"

"I did not." This information calmed him in a startling descent from anger. Armand lowered his hands and then splayed them before him in a gesture of understanding. "Forgive me."

"I ask not for your pity."

"And you'll not receive it." He gripped her by the wrist and escorted her over the threshold, where he lifted her bag and shoved it into her hands. "I'll give you five minutes."

She looked away from his retreat, fighting the wave of tears that vied to flood over her cheeks. There was nothing more to say. She'd been discovered. Armand would believe only what was so obviously evident.

The slam of his chamber door made her jump.

He could not say that she would have ever used sex to lure

the information from him. Yes, Fouquet had planned it that way. To which she had only reluctantly agreed. But it hadn't worked that way. Her body hadn't cared a whit for keeping an inheritance intact, no, it had reacted to Armand of its own volition. Madeleine had wanted Armand. To be in his arms and lose all control. For while Madeleine had come into Armand's life as the enemy, she now only wanted to be protected and loved by him.

Sides had been crossed. Desire and emotion had been introduced.

And with that daring play, she had lost.

Hours later the carriage stopped at the Porte St. Germaine while the coachman waited for a caravan of gypsy wagons to produce papers before traveling through the city gates. Great blazing torches were lined along the wall, a beacon to travelers.

Silence had gagged like a thick wadding of cloth in Madeleine's throat during the entirety of the journey. After shuffling her across Vaux's construction grounds to the stables and demanding she sit silent in the carriage seat opposite him, Armand had then pulled his hat brim over his eyes and settled into the corner of the seat. Most likely he had not been snoozing during their travel, but instead keeping a keen ear upon her every movement.

The carriage began to wobble upon its wheels and pass between the forboding walls fortressed around the grand city.

Madeleine felt stiff and tense. And desperate.

In but moments, Armand would leave her life. It mattered not that she faced prosecution as a spy; all Madeleine could think was that she'd not see Armand ever again. His voice would never again slide over her flesh and seduce her to submission. Nor would his mere presence conquer her and make her think of passion and kisses and bodies intertwined in ways she'd never thought possible.

Oh, that she had not made love with him! If only she could prolong these last few moments, even if spent in silence. She had to attempt it.

"I know I've stepped over a line that should have never been crossed. I've betrayed you. But I never imagined I'd love the man I would hurt."

"You use the word too easily, Madame."

Word? She knew he meant *love*. And that he could not speak it told her much about him.

"You speak of things that can never truly be possessed," Armand offered in such a knowing hush that Madeleine's hopes slipped from her thoughts and floated out the window.

What knowledge did he have of unpossessable love? And why did he speak of it with such knowing?

She jerked her head up, though the night darkened the interior of the carriage to a haze of moving shadows. "Will I spend the night in the Bastille?"

"I cannot guess. I shall leave you in the capable hands of Captain Lambert. If you remember, I've a mission, and its success depends on secrecy. A secrecy you have breached, Madame. So now, time is of the essence."

"Will I see you again?"

The coach stopped, and Armand jumped out and lowered the folding steps. His hand jutted inside the carriage, awaiting her to follow.

"I must know," she said, unable to release her iron clutch on the leather cushion beneath her thighs. "If only you would give me a moment of your time—"

"I've surrendered days of my time all in the name of your silly games, Madame."

She could not see his face, but the tension in his voice cut through her heart like a warrior's blade. "But I need to explain."

"About what? The sick father? The dead husband? Or perhaps your lover, Fouquet?"

"He is not my lover!"

Now Madeleine stepped down and marched ahead toward the steps that queued up to the musketeer headquarters. That Armand could even think she could be involved with Fouquet in such a way!

"I did not want to hurt you," she hissed, though she figured her defense fruitless by now.

Armand's sure grip clamped onto one of her wrists. Not possessive, more aggressive. "Fortunately, you have not hurt me," he rasped, as they landed the top step and entered the quiet halls. "But it remains to be seen what harm you have brought to this mission. Now I request your silence, Madame. Grant me that one mercy as a sign of retribution for your betrayals."

But with her silence he would never learn the truth behind her desperation.

That she had brought this fate, this horrid loss of a new love, upon herself was evident. Madeleine had gotten herself into a terrible mess.

She was on her own now.

Pray Stephan would not suffer for her mistake.

Patience had fled. The armor that had once surrounded his heart had been shined and replaced with tight screws. No longer would he allow himself to succumb to Madeleine's charms or her whispered adorations and her damned betrayals!

Damn! Why had he not known?

Nervous energy, combined with an uncomfortable trace of regret surged through Armand's system as he exited the Louvre. Armand had come directly there after leaving Madeleine in Captain Lambert's surprised hands. Colbert had to be roused from sleep, but he was beyond delight to look over the papers Armand had absconded from Fouquet's private files. Indeed, they were in code. It would take Colbert a three-candle night to look through them, so Armand could but go home and wait for word that his mission had been a success.

But he was too high-strung to sit at home. Armand just could not figure this. If Fouquet suspected Armand was spying on him, then why not just eliminate him instead of planting a spy? What a complicated plan. It didn't make sense. Nothing made sense. Most of all, his conflicted emotions made the least sense.

He hastened his footsteps and mounted his horse in a smooth leap. Jabbing his spurs into the beast's flanks he navigated the narrow aisles of Paris's dark streets. When the musketeer headquarters passed on his right, he did not glance at the one lighted window in the building. A jab of his spur coaxed his horse onward, not slowing for patrons, only hoping they would rush out of harm's way.

The horse's hooves beat a hollow clopping rhythm upon the cobbles, dampening the intrusive thoughts that spiked Armand's brain. Focused only on getting away, far, far away from this confusing crossroad he found himself at, Armand clicked his tongue, beckoning his journey faster and faster.

He passed through the Porte Montemartre with nary a glance from the gatekeeper. Metallic gray sky spiked by black treetops surrounded the city. The creak of a windmill's sails barely rounding its axle for the lack of wind seemed to holler, "*Adieu,* you are leaving this wretched city!"

Wretched indeed. Gritting his teeth and wrapping the leather reins about his gloved fist, Armand urged his mount into a gallop upon the packed high road that led west, and eventually dropped into the sea. A long ride off, the sea, but almost inviting.

Almost.

The fierce cadence of horse hooves beating the road wakened the memories in Armand's sealed repository of the past. Hard and fast and destined for freedom, always the pace of horse hooves reminded him of escape.

And once again Armand found himself seeking escape.

A shout burst from his throat; a release of pent-up energy. He flung the reins aside and spread his arms out wide. Lifting his face to the heavens, he closed his eyes. Warm night air brisked over his flesh, raked through his hair and pressed his clothing close to his body. He clung to the horse's muscled torso with his thighs, knowing the animal would continue to soar across the landscape without pause for direction from a mere human. For the horse sought escape as well. Freedom from constant direction, from a life spent serving others.

Escape from everything.

Armand sought escape from his past. Escape from the future. Escape from life.

Ah, escape. To be free like this, soaring through the sky with the power of a great beast beneath him and no destination save the comfort of a clear mind. It didn't feel so terrible, rather freeing—but cold.

I am chilled. His heart shivered in response to his inner thoughts. *I do not like this. I've had the freedom granted by your greed. I want nothing more of it.*

Stunned at this sudden revelation, Armand slipped his fingers through the horse's mane and brought the sweating stallion to a halt in the middle of the road. Darkness surrounded, but did not blind. Darkness had once been Armand's partner in crime. If he'd not held a shiver in his bones as he'd anticipated the approaching booty, the night was not mature enough for success.

There was no moon tonight, at least not that he could see through the hazy clouds. And but a handful of Madame Medusa's stars. Dark enough for mischief.

Dark enough for the crime of betrayal.

Armand slid from his mount and kicked the road, but no dust rose at his boot toe, for the constant traffic traveling from Paris to the country had packed the surface to a hard crust. Hands on hips, his head down, his eyes not really seeing, he paced the road.

Indeed, his greed had provided a certain *form* of freedom. It had granted him the security in knowing his family would not starve. It had laid fine clothing upon his shoulders and strung handsome frippery around his wrists and neck and boot tops to attract the ladies. Of course, ladies had only been considered for one thing—their qualifications. Naïveté. Widow. Rich.

Such as the Countess de Bleu. He'd arranged to accidentally meet her at the Opera, introduced himself as a Spanish baron traveling to England who had been robbed and was in need of a room to spend a few days before his family could forward funds to him. The countess would not think of a fine man such as himself spending the night in a dirty, lice-infested inn. Armand had spent a week charming her, and though he had acted the grateful but undeserving lover, she had lined his pockets with enough jewelry to see him to England and back a hundred times.

There was Marriette d'Blige, also recently widowed, but with a greedy eye for the court fops. She liked her men to wear a specific shade of green—she called it pistachio—and a scarlet mouche on the left cheek to prove their devotion to her. But when the fabric she required for her amour's uniforms ran out, Armand convinced her that he could travel to Italy and bring back rolls and rolls of the cherished silk. Traveling expenses and a handsome stipend had been provided. Armand had yet to set foot in Italy.

Ariel, Madame de Bernier, the wicked-tongued Duvette, and others too numerous to name had all showered him with coin and jewel after a well-orchestrated performance and not a few nights in bed.

Had he enjoyed it all?

Some.

To be truthful? Yes, most certainly all.

Until Valérie.

Armand kicked a rock that sat in a tuft of grass sprouting at the edge of the road.

That his greed had granted him freedom was a given. But that it had also granted guilt, regret, and stripped the honor from the Saint-Sylvestre name could not be ignored. He'd not spared a moment of thought for the honor of his family's name when he'd been slipping the jewels from a wealthy widow's neck. How could he even invoke his father's memory when he knew the man would be sickened to know his son had taken to such devious methods to support his children?

"Can I ever receive the forgiveness I seek?" Armand said into the velvet night sky. "I am so sorry, Father!"

He fell to his knees and pounded his fists into the grass. Twilight dew moistened his lace-rimmed sleeves. He did not want to change the past. He could not. For if he had chosen to join a regiment twelve years ago instead of stealing coin, it would have been necessary to send Mignonne and Adrian to an orphanage. Alexandre, too, most likely, for he was but thirteen then. They could not have survived on their own, and with but the paltry wages a soldier received.

"I did what was necessary," Armand pleaded with the heavens. "I did not take what was not offered to me."

Yes, he had deceived, but still . . .

"I am prepared to suffer my fate unending. I have turned away from the life that I so adored. The clothing on my back is but all I own. I would sell it for a suit of plain cloth and worn boots in a moment if only things could be different."

But how different? The past could not be changed. The future—yes, his future.

He had held it in his hands, caressed the soft tendrils of his future's hair, breathed in the amber scent of her soul, without even knowing it at the time.

And tonight he had locked that future away just as he had wrapped the chains about his heart years ago. And the chains he had given to Madeleine tonight would not protect her; indeed, they might harm her.

Tap, tap.

Armand startled. What? There was that odd tapping noise again. Inside his head. He'd heard it before when he'd been relaxed and content, enjoying Madeleine's company. And even the night of his fateful wedding vows. But was it really in his head?

Tap, tap.

So odd . . . it was almost as if—could it be?

Why, the woman had opened the rusted lock and had successfully broached the interior. Impossible! Armand forced a frown. He did not have a care for this spy. Did he? Could he? But that would mean . . .

The tapping had ceased. Now the sensation of warmth wrapping round his heart overwhelmed. Damn, how perplexing! It was Madeleine that made him feel this way, all warm and even a little bit mellow. But this was impossible. She was the enemy! This was not supposed to happen!

"Why did she deceive me?"

She had tried to tell him her reasons, but he would not hear it, so consumed by anger had he been.

Armand now sensed there was some piece missing from this puzzle, a large piece that he still had not touched. But it was the piece needed to bridge the gap between his and Madeleine's pieces on the large board of life, he knew that much.

Tonight Captain Lambert would see her to the dungeon below the Louvre, where she would stay until she could be questioned in the morning. That she would have to endure the horrors of that filthy place for one night!

"What have I done?" Armand stood and turned back to his horse, a fierce silhouette against the distant glow of Paris. The city of light beckoned now with its aura of gold. Since ancient times, Paris had held the nickname for the light that emanated from its bosom. Somewhere deep beneath that arc of inviting light the woman he cared for was being placed in manacles.

Yes, he did care for her! No matter what Madeleine had done. Hadn't he done the same in the past? For the first time in his life Armand had touched that elusive feeling; he felt that gentle tapping at his heart, and now it would not allow him to escape its lure.

"I've not heard everything from Madeleine. And until I do, I must not judge her." He raced to his stallion and mounted. With a heel to its flanks and a jerk of the reins, he headed back to Paris.

There was a damsel in dire need of rescue.

Twelve

The windows in the shadowed gray-brick facade of musketeer headquarters were all black, the dirty glass reflecting the moon that had peeked out from the clouds as Armand rode back to the city. It must be later than he had thought, for it was a rare night that saw the barracks silent before the morning hour.

Heels treading the cobbles suddenly clicked into hearing range, and Armand was alerted to the alley to the right of the building, which spit out a whistling young cadet swinging his dagger on the tip of his finger.

"Monsieur!"

The cadet snapped into a defensive posture, his eyes scanning the darkness and his dagger held ready. "Who goes there?"

"Armand Saint-Sylvestre, cadet in the seventh foot." His horse pawed the ground, jangling the metal fixings on its reins and exhaling puffs of breath through its nose. "I did not mean to startle you, I am only in search of Captain Lambert."

"You just missed him, Monsieur. He left for home with a prisoner in hand. Fetching young thing."

"He did not have plans to bring her to the Louvre?"

"No, Monsieur. I spoke to him myself."

His home? Interesting. Armand had to wonder what Min would think when her husband crossed the threshold with Madame Medusa in hand. His sister was not taken to sharing her man with anyone.

"Thank you, Monsieur." Armand flicked the brim of his hat and turned his mount the direction he had come.

Captain Lambert lived on the left bank, as did he, not far from the boatmen's calls on the Seine. Passing few mounted riders and even fewer on foot, Armand rounded the narrow street that led to the captain's house and spied the twosome when a flash of moon glow fell upon Madeleine's violet skirts.

Heeling his mount to a trot, Armand was stunned to see that Captain Lambert pulled Madeleine protectively to his side with Armand's approach. The sight stung Armand in the heart.

"Armand," Madeleine cried, then she uttered an "oh," as if she suddenly recalled it was he that had turned her over for her crimes, and she should not be so excited to see him.

"Saint-Sylvestre," Chance said, and pushed away from Madeleine's side. "Forget something?"

"You are taking her to your home?"

The captain approached as Armand slid off his horse. Chance doffed his hat and tucked it under his arm. He spoke quietly, once eyeing Madeleine, who stood by the brick wall of his building, to ensure she could not hear. "I had to rescue your sister from the filthy dungeons of the Louvre once, if you remember. I'll not put another female there anytime soon."

"That is kind of you." That he had left Madeleine in good hands was now evident, beyond the twinge of jealousy Armand had just felt at seeing Chance holding his wife so close. "I've changed my mind, I don't wish to turn Madeleine over to you."

"You—ha!" Chance clamped him heartily across the shoulders. "It doesn't work that way, Saint-Sylvestre. I've filled out the papers, arranged for an interrogation in the morning—"

"Lose the papers." Accustomed to drawing steel to make a point, Armand cautioned his instincts to remain at heel. He did not lay a hand upon his sword, but instead sharpened his voice. "She was forced to commit the crime of spying. I know if I can but talk to her, the truth will be known. Please, Captain—Chance, I will be her guard tonight."

"Oh, I don't think so, brother-in-law. I can wager how much guarding you'll be doing with this beauty in your bed."

Armand glanced to Madeleine. Her hands were tied before her with rough, grimy rope. She did not look up to him, only stared at the ground, accepting her fate. His porcelain doll had been broken.

No. She was going nowhere but with him tonight.

"I will not walk away, but with Madeleine in hand."

"You jeopardize your commission, Saint-Sylvestre."

"Damn the commission! Madeleine means more to me than my own life."

Even through the gray haze of the early-morning hour, Armand could see the lift of Chance's brow and the grin that fought to wipe away his staunch grimace. The captain crossed his arms before him and planted his feet at a wide stance, silently urging Armand to elaborate.

"You would do the same for Min," Armand said. "You know you would not allow her to suffer an interrogation if she were innocent."

"But your wife is not innocent. The very fact that she is your wife proves her alliances with Fouquet."

"One day," Armand insisted. "Misplace those damned papers for but a day. I shall keep Madeleine in hand and interrogate her myself. If I find that she is indeed guilty of allying herself with Fouquet, I promise you I will bring her to the Louvre and fire the torture weapons to a blaze myself."

The captain raised a finger to protest, then stalled. "You're just as stubborn as your sister, you know that?"

Armand inclined a positive nod and shrug at the captain.

"Very well." Captain Lambert glanced up the apartment building where a window reflected the inner light of a waiting candle. "I'm not so sure Min will take to a female guest tonight as it is. But one day," he warned as he walked over to Madeleine and pulled her forward by the ropes that bound her wrists.

Armand reclaimed his wife with an arm around her waist. He said a few more thank-yous to the captain, then boosted Madeleine up onto his horse.

"Guard your back, Saint-Sylvestre," the captain called as Armand mounted behind Madeleine. "The squirrel dashes from one tree to another with agility and ease. Do not allow him to win you over to his side with the lure of a pretty face and promises of false love."

Armand did not answer, only heeled his horse and galloped into the night.

"It isn't far," he whispered into the intoxicating amber streams of Madeleine's hair.

"I'm all right. But my hands, this rope burns."

Armand drew out his rapier, reached around, and sliced through the rope. "I'm sorry. For everything." Brushing away the coarse hemp, he lifted one of her hands up and leaned forward over her shoulder to press a long kiss to the hot welt. "How cruel. Your skin is so delicate."

Her body eased against his torso, her head seeming to want to fall back and rest upon his shoulder, but she did not allow it. Words gasped from her lips as quickly as the timorous heartbeats Armand could feel beat against his chest. "Why did you do it? Come back for me?"

"I should have listened to you earlier, allowed you to explain. Often my anger makes me shortsighted. But I want to listen to you now, Madeleine. If you can forgive my rash behavior earlier."

"There is nothing to forgive. You were only doing your job. But trust me, I would have never purposely chosen to do such a thing. Not to you. Oh." She wavered and Armand caught her body tight against his. Now she did allow her head to find rest upon his shoulder. "I'm so tired. The day has been trying."

"My home is not far. I will give you this night to rest, and we will speak of this in the morning."

"Thank you, Armand."

And with the clasp of her fingers around his own, Armand knew he had done the right thing.

The apartment was small and sparely furnished. The hearthroom sported but one rush-matted chair and a small stool covered with a ragged tapestry. A beaten cupboard held a tin plate and tankard and indeterminable utensils. Armand did not seem to mind the living conditions as he strode across the room, depositing his sword on the mantel and joining the tiny space as if a missing piece returned.

"You may sleep in my bedchamber. The rug before the hearth will serve me well enough."

She glanced to the rug, a wide oval of thick creamy wool. Madeleine didn't even think to argue. She was exhausted, her shoulders ached after an afternoon spent being jostled about in the carriage, and her hindquarters throbbed after their trip from Captain Lambert's home. Sleep was quite necessary.

A refreshing cloak of cool air settled upon Madeleine's shoulders as she followed Armand into the bedroom. The darkness burst into a golden glow as he lit a candle sitting in an iron holder on the knee-high stool near his bed. Madeleine was immediately attracted to the royal blue counterpane spread neatly across the feather mattress.

What might have once been slippery satin had been worn to a soft spread of still-rich blue, embroidered over with starbursts in gold-and-copper threading. Worn, but that of dreams of sultans and Arabian princesses that had peopled Madeleine's childhood fairy stories. Now she thought the blanket would be most delicious swaddled about a sweet infant crooked in her arms.

"It's beautiful."

Like a warm desert storm, she felt Armand's presence envelop her from behind. "I have had this old rag for decades." His voice dripped of precious memories and admiration. "I cannot part with it. Maman made it for me when I was but a child. I once considered having the tattered backing resewn with new fabric, but I couldn't bring myself to leave it with the seamstress for the fortnight she required. Silly thing."

"No." Not for a blanket that resembled a midnight sky gilded with stars.

"I'm tired, as I'm sure you are," he said, and Madeleine heard the door creak behind her. "I'll see you tomorrow morn."

"Thank you, Armand." He turned to her, and she added, "For trusting me."

"I do not trust, only care." With a nod, he dismissed her and closed the door.

She pulled the bows in her bodice free from their tight knots. What she wouldn't pay for a maid right now. Someone to strip her down to her chemise, pull a warm wet towel across her limbs, and comb through her hair, while she sat in a somnambulant lull upon the rich blanket of dreams.

From the window she scanned the tiled red rooftops across the narrow street, and spied St. Séverin's steeple poking the gunmetal sky in the distance. A noisy quarter peopled with artisans and intellectuals, St. Germaine also hosted soldiers who preferred to distance themselves from the Louvre's tight quarters. It was fitting that Armand had sequestered himself from the military. It must be difficult for him to make the change from his past to what he now did. Of course, Madeleine did not consider spying much of a leap from thievery. But spying sanctioned by the military was a step up.

Interesting that he'd chosen such a profession. She wondered now if it was because he could never really leave the excitement of the chase behind, or if there were another reason entirely. What she wouldn't give to know Armand Saint-Sylvestre's mind. What made this man make the choices he had made? Why had he stolen when he seemed too far distant from any criminal she had ever seen about at the Bastille?

And why had he come back for her tonight? Truly, this man was one of many facets.

Did he really mean what he'd just said? That he cared?

"I want to know you, Armand," she said, as she stripped off her stays and skirts, and rolled her hose down each leg, depositing them in a crumpled pile upon the floor. "There is so much I want to tell you. I . . . I need help."

Yes, she had to admit, she did need help. No longer could she do this all on her own. And Armand was the only one who could get her out of the mess Fouquet had stirred her into.

With a wistful sigh, Madeleine ran her fingers through her hair and decided she'd seek out a washbasin in the morning. Sleep demanded she heed its call.

The snap of a crackling fire told her Armand had just enough energy to make his own cozy nest for the night. She touched the azure counterpane, scrunched the worn satin in her fist. *I could not part with it . . .*

Seeing Armand through his childhood memories painted over the cold facts Fouquet had given her. Surely from what she had seen of the man—for he had been honorable enough to agree to remain in this marriage even knowing he'd been tricked—Armand had had good reason for committing the crimes of his past.

Madeleine scooped the heavy blanket into her arms and, clad only in her chemise, padded barefoot across the cool pine flooring to the main room, where a single-log fire glowed in blood-and-orange licks. Armand lay sprawled on his side before the bewitching flames. Surely he did not yet sleep. Though, for as tired as she felt, it was very possible.

His eyes were closed, his hands cupped near his chin. He'd not even removed his boots. A blossom of crimson sat upon his well-muscled biceps like a flower petal fallen from the sky. Too proud he'd been to let her nurse him, as most men were.

No, that hadn't been so. He'd been too angry to allow her to touch him after what he'd heard in Fouquet's study.

"Forgive me," she whispered. "I never wanted to hurt you."

Madeleine spread the blanket of dreams over his body, touched his arm to find the wound had already crusted and was small in diameter. She straightened to quietly tiptoe away— but Armand reached out and clasped the hem of her chemise.

"Thank you," he offered in a sleep-heavy voice.

Kneeling beside him, Madeleine spread her hand over the blanket, unable to resist the raised stitching and timeworn texture. "Your mother gifted you with the heavens. I can understand why you couldn't part with such a treasure. I should think a new backing would destroy the love she wove in every stitch."

At Armand's gesture, Madeleine lay beside him on the thick sheep's wool rug, and he pulled the blanket to cover her as well. He rolled onto his back, his bootheels rubbing on the floor. The fire flashed red in the waves of his dark hair, put a warm blush in his cheeks, and glittered in his eyes.

"I think I was five when she made me this blanket. Yes, I believe so, because Mignonne had not yet been born, though Maman carried her in her belly. She died giving birth to my sister. I hated that little baby for the longest time after."

He closed his eyes, grimaced, then smiled a knowing, generous smile. "But when Min started toddling about, getting into my things, and playing with my abandoned wooden swords, I could hardly continue to despise *ma petite.*"

Madeleine found Armand's hand beneath the blanket and slipped her fingers through his. He squeezed and turned to press a fleeting kiss to the tip of her nose.

"Tell me about her," Madeleine whispered. "Your mother."

He turned his head to stare up at the fire shadows rippling across the dark-beamed ceiling. "She was the most beautiful woman in the entire world. Still is."

Madeleine sensed his smile. He was tired, but relaxed, and more than willing to share this small glimpse of his life with her.

"Papa met her in his travels through Spain. She was from Andalusia, and wore her long black hair straight down her back. She always smelled a certain way. I never knew the name of the scent, but it was in everything she wore, everything she created." He lifted the blanket to his nose. "It's not here anymore . . . her scent. But it lives in my heart, like an exotic flower that lives hidden in a thick forest, blooming only under the light of the full moon, and only for a moment. Like that flower, Maman's life was too brief."

Snaps of brilliant orange spark burst into the air and landed but inches from where they lay, to fizzle to glowing dust.

"She used to dance . . ." Again the smile returned to his voice. "It was an Andulusian dance, she would tell me. She hadn't the proper instruments to create the music, but it played in her memory. She'd tell me that, too. Maman would dance outside on the lawn in her long red dress with the horses cantering in the distance. So pretty she was with her hair hanging wild over her shoulders and her long arms stretched gracefully above her head. She'd twist her wrists and play the story with her fingers and gentle movements of her hips. I could sit for hours watching her, seduced by a culture that had been lost to her after marrying Papa. But she loved him so that she'd always say she'd have followed him all the way to the savage frontier of the Americas if he'd asked."

"She sounds a marvel," Madeleine said. "It is good you have such vivid memories of her. And this."

She spread her hands over the blanket, thinking the only tokens from her childhood were intangible memories. A knowing image of a man with arms extended and large square hands, perhaps her father. Perhaps not. A perfect black tulip grown in a gilded pot given her on her sixteenth birthday. Again, suspicious of her father's hand, but she knew less than little about the man. He was a virtual apparition. Still the memories were always there, and they were treasures, just as this blanket was a treasure to Armand.

He seemed to grasp her thoughts and open them to his own. "You said your mother is in Venice?"

"We have not been close for years."

Cecile hadn't even attended her first wedding ceremony. Though, upon hearing of Madeleine's inheritance, she had come for a two-day visit, leaving with a healthy stipend. Just until she could secure her position in the Duke de Metaninni's heart, Cecile had reassured. He'd gifted her with a palazzo, but no allowance even for clothing. "We had some nice times as well when I was little."

Armand turned on his side to face her and drew his forefinger along her cheek, pushing aside a tickling curl of hair. "Tell me."

"Oh, well, I've told you that mother was the Duchess le Reaux's handmaid. But she would have the evenings to spend with me because the duchess believed in lying down before the sun set. That would allow us a few hours before we ourselves went to bed. Cecile would allow me to mend the duchess's gown, and occasionally we'd giggle over silly things, like which prince stumbled upon his heels before the king, or which marquis was rumored to be holding a certain peasant's favors."

"You call her Cecile?"

"Yes, well ..." How could one really invoke the title of mother when she'd never once felt love or protection or even more than casual interest from that person?

"It's a pity the duchess could not see to your dowry, for all your mother's years of service. Ah ... but the lack of dowry was a ruse. How quickly I forget you've woven a masterful tale, Madame Medusa.''

"Yes,'' Madeleine murmured, wishing desperately the conversation had not suddenly turned to her betrayals.

"Was Papa even a relative?''

"No. I don't wish to discuss this.''

"Of course we should not now when there is the morning for that. But you understand my curiosity?''

"I do. But you mustn't worry about me. After we part ways, I'll fare as well as ever.''

"I would like to believe that.''

She blinked. No pretense to his voice, not a hint of the sloe-eyed charm, just a genuine heartfelt statement. They touched gazes in the vibrant glow of firelight. Armand's look reached out and embraced Madeleine in a soul-sheltering hug. So unlike anything she'd ever received from her mother.

He drew his fingers over her hair in exploratory design. He kissed her on the jaw. Once. Twice. Soft, and sweet. And silence followed.

Madeleine lay still for the longest time, running Armand's words through her mind as the crackles of wood silenced to simmering hisses, and his soft breathing became deeper and more relaxed as sleep captured him. The faint scent of blood from his wound and dust from the high roads combined with the burned ash in a curious perfume.

Armand's head became heavy upon her shoulder, his arm, lying across her stomach, felt weighty, but welcome. Their contact was beyond the overt intimacy they'd shared over the past few days. It went beyond deep kisses and naked flesh and daring touches here and there, and to places on his body she'd not yet seen.

Lying on the floor in front of the simmering fire with her husband's arm draped across her body and the blanket of dreams covering their limbs felt as perfect as any wish could ever be.

And this was no wish, it was reality.

A reality that would cease to exist after she had exposed all.

But until the sun rose, Madeleine intended to enjoy every moment to its fullest. She closed her eyes and snuggled close to the warmth of Armand's body.

Tap, tap . . .

You cannot ignore me. I've touched you! Your heart shall never be the same. I've torn away the fetters and grasped hold. You feel it, do not deny it!

Armand startled awake. He blinked in the darkness. The fire still crackled, its wild flames calmed to infrequent licks, but it was another warmth that filled him—the warmth of another.

Madeleine snored gently at his side, her hand sprawled across his stomach. He stroked the narrow lengths of her fingers. Her freckled knuckles had been rapping at his heart again, reminding him that it had been captured, and she'd no interest in releasing him.

Madeleine was not an evil soul. Only she'd become involved with an evil that was no match for her spirit. He wanted to help her. He needed to help her, for if he did not, he would lose her. And he could not lose the woman who had claimed his heart. He would find a way to wrench her away from Fouquet's clutches and convince Captain Lambert she had been forced to spy.

She was *his* Madame Medusa. And he liked having her saucy smile and catty blue eyes in his life. He liked the feel of her body pressed alongside his, the swish of her garnet hair tracing his lips.

And he still wanted *anything*. Though, he wanted it without condition now. She did not need him to remain married to her for the sake of an ailing father. That had been a well-planned farce to trap him into this marriage. And he did not need her to satisfy those urges he'd ignored so long.

No, he needed Madeleine for the renewal of spirit she had

given him these past few days. Madeleine's quiet allure had triumphed over Medusa's seductions. The fire he had sought in his adventures as a spy had been found in the glitter of a pair of catty blue eyes.

He slipped his hand over the worn blanket and corraled a thick clasp of her hair in his fingers. Like liquid fire, swirling and twining and consuming his desire. He wanted to cling to her as long as she would allow.

"I love you, Madeleine," he whispered into the darkness, aware that she was sleeping and could not hear his confession. "I know that I do."

Thick curls fell from his palm as she stirred and turned over to lie on her back; Armand followed the wave of her body as if a tidal force beckoning him to remain in sync. Her flesh was warm, supple, fragrant under his roaming touch as he glided up her arm and traced the elegant line of her shoulder to the curve at the base of her neck.

Another rustle of her legs, a tilt of her head, and she whispered, "Is it morning?"

"Still far away."

"I don't want to leave you, Armand. Hold me."

He pressed against her and kissed her eyelids, her lashes tickling his nose. Their bodies meshed together as if two silver serving spoons lying upon a dinner table. They fit perfectly.

"I want to hold you always, Madeleine."

"Tomorrow we will be parted."

That depended on whether he decided to play the honorable soldier or the lovesick spy. "We still have this night."

Their kisses began slowly. Neither spoke as they shed their clothes. When Armand stood in but his underbreeches and Madeleine her ribboned chemise, she pulled back from his kisses and gripped the fabric near her hips. Holding desperately to his dark eyes, she pulled the chemise high until the heat of the flames warmed the heavy globes of her breasts. She slipped it over her head and let it flutter to the floor behind her. Armand's tongue dashed out to lick his lower lip.

Standing proudly, Madeleine smoothed her palms over her body, drawing with her actions Armand's intense interest. This was no performance. This was complete truth.

She cupped her breasts, finding them achy with the need for Armand's mouth. Her stomach, smooth and flat, prickled to thousands of shiver bumps as her fingers glided lower.

It felt good, standing before the hungry eyes of a dangerously dark spy who could not speak save for the need in his eyes, the flinch of his fingers, the quickening rasps of his breath. Spreading her fingers up through her hair, Madeleine pulled the long tresses out to full length and slowly released the ends, reveling in the sensuous feel of her hair across her flesh.

Behind them a sharp crackle snapped an ember from the hearth.

"Have I turned you to stone?" she asked teasingly, as she twisted a thick curl around her fingertip.

Armand held out a hand, his fingers beckoning. "Why don't you come see."

He laid her hand over his loins. Madeleine pressed her body to his, her nipples rigid against his hot bare chest, her hips kissing his and her fingers caressing his member through the soft wool underbreeches. "Hard as stone," she whispered.

"Once again, Madame Medusa succeeds in her accidental seduction. No more teasing. I've been a good boy. I've waited and restrained myself, it's time for my reward."

"Anything?"

"And more." He lowered her to the blanket and straddled her body.

Madeleine reached up to trace his broad chest. His nipples were rosy and hard, tiny reproductions of her own. Hooking her fingers at each side of Armand's underbreeches she shimmied them down his hips and over his firm buttocks. Leaving

him to wiggle them over his ankles and off, she cupped his
hard muscles and pressed him closer.

He felt so good. Feverish and hard, and very different from
her own flesh. This man was forged of fire and pride, and she
liked the feel of his body skimming under her palms. And the
delicious tones that moved over his lips. Every moan that
tripped from his mouth hummed deep within her, like an inner
music that resonated touch and emotion.

He hovered above her, spreading his fingers through her hair,
arranging the long streams of copper and crimson across the
blanket. Armand's eyes, his devoted attention to her, reflected
a beauty she had not known until now.

With Armand's masterful touch, Madeleine found the woman
she had become that night of the king's party. A woman that
had been hidden by years of ridicule and neglect at court.
The woman that had been further chastened and hidden after
suffering a disastrous wedding night.

Now that newly born woman could think of nothing but
satisfying urges and fulfilling dreams of passion long imagined.

Threading her fingers through Armand's raven-feather hair,
she pulled him into her kiss. He held her so tight she thought
she'd faint. He kissed her so hard she thought she'd see bruises
in the morning. But he made her feel so right, that she could
not stop.

"Tell me," he rasped, "were you frightened that night at
Versailles when I had you on the bed and was so close to
having you?" He did not wait for a response, so set on his
intentions as he took her nipple into his mouth.

"A little." Her voice ended on a high note at the touch of
his wet tongue to her breast.

"You were playing a part, eh?"

Madeleine tried desperately to reason the situation, but it
was impossible with this man drawing such exquisite sensations
to the surface of her flesh. "You already know. Why do you
bring this up again?"

He paused and looked up, his dark irises surrounded by perfect white. "I just want to know if it is another part you play now?"

"Oh no." She relaxed and straightened beneath him. "I play no part other than that of a willing and desirous wife. Take me, Armand. Make me your wife in every way. You make me feel as if I am the only woman in the world." She trailed a finger over his lips. "When I know there have probably been dozens before me."

"Don't speak of the past," he cautioned, gripping her finger and kissing the length of it up and down until he landed in her palm and traced his tongue along what seemed like each and every line. "It is the present moment and the walk into the future that makes you exactly what you wish to be. And right now, Madeleine, you are the only woman in the world. My queen of accidental seduction."

She giggled and suddenly arched her back as he laved one of her nipples.

"I don't for a minute believe you actually have a thumb on what you really want," he said as he lowered his head and kissed her between the breasts. "But as soon as you've hit on something—"

"You mean *anything?*"

"Yes, anything—you triumph."

"Works for me."

"As well for me."

His hips began to rock against hers and his kisses slipped greedily along her neck, strafing her with an intense chord of need. Need to rise and release.

She gripped his deliciously muscled buttocks and followed his rhythm. Slipping each leg to the side allowed him contact with the tender folds of her garden. Medusa's victim, solid as marble, slithed up and down, slickening itself upon her wetness.

"I must be inside you," he gasped in her ear.

"Yes, now."

Her husband's heavy entrance forced Madeleine's hips high to bond with him, and she arced her head deep into the wool rug. She clawed her fingertips along his back and felt her nipples rub against his chest. All paled as his length filled her with a heat more dazzling than the fire radiating beside them. Tight and slippery and so different, it felt. He filled her; she enveloped him. Together they moved to a rhythm new to Madeleine, yet it came to her as if an ancient tribal chant thrummed into her senses. Over and over they danced to the beat, their mouths sucking each other's lips, chin, shoulders. Moans of ecstatic desperation filled the room as they danced upon the blanket of the heavens.

A vivid coil began to tighten deep in Madeleine's loins. It strung from her throat to her gut and down to her curled toes, until it filled her senses with an intense want, a need to rush forward, spring out and up, and perhaps even . . . fly.

Held tight by Armand, she noticed him shuddering as his rhythms increased to hard and steady beats. *Yes,* she wanted to scream, *I can feel freedom so close. Don't stop!* But her voice was abandoned in favor of her soul's powerful communication with Armand's soul.

And he let out a moan, freezing inside her momentarily, as his strong arms supported him above her. Armand fed her womb with a hot stream of seed, the rush of heat and realization of his climax teasing her to the edge. Flight began. Madeleine cried Armand's name.

She could not grasp the sensation. Bliss shimmered within her in every tint of the rainbow. An altogether unexplainable phenomenon had just occured between her and her husband.

And there was only one way to reason it, or even acknowledge the intensity of emotion that welled in heavy tears and spilled over Madeleine's cheeks. "I love you, Armand."

Thirteen

Morning proved that as much as a warm body and soft blanket had seemed a pleasant way to sleep, a hard floor was not. Slowly sitting upright, Madeleine eased her hand down her back where cords of muscles protested her decision not to sleep in bed. The azure blanket still covered her legs, but Armand was gone. She pricked her ears, but did not hear him in the bedchamber; nor were there signs of his boots or sword in the room in which she sat.

Judging from the beam of sunlight that sat horizontal to her sight in the sky, she figured it to be late. Where was he? They'd made perfect love last night. It should be topped by a perfect morning spent languishing in his arms. Armand had made her his wife in every sense of the word. He had joined with her. And it had been beyond dreams.

Madeleine pushed her fingers up through her hair, got caught up in the snarls, and then with a sigh, said a silent thank-you that Armand was not around. She must look a horror. And if she looked anywhere near as awful as her back felt, it was a good thing she was alone.

Unless he had gone to fetch his captain and have her taken away in manacles.

No, he could not dream to do such a thing after making love to her. Last night he had changed his mind. They'd plans to talk this morning. She wanted to reveal how Fouquet had blackmailed her into doing his bidding.

I love you.

She'd said those words last night as the incredible flight of passion had lifted her soul into the infinity. And she'd meant them.

Perhaps Armand would someday return the sentiment. Oh, he must. She wished it to be so. Her shoulder slumped. Ah, but wishing was not the same as being. Armand was not here for a reason.

Why?

Frills and frippery laced the walls and floors and ceiling of Lady de Winter's Fashionable Boutique. Armand could not take a single step without being brushed by a bouffant of feathers and ticklers, or tripping up on a mountain of beribboned and pearled pillows. A headache was imminent for the mixture of scents that assaulted him from every corner.

This morning, while Madeleine had snored—such a sweet racket!—Armand had risen and skipped downstairs. Bread and ale from his landlord's wife appeased his hunger, but he'd wanted something more tasty for Madeleine. Fresh cheese and wine. That would be perfect.

Madeleine was a beautiful woman, sensuous and witty. Once he'd figured that it was she who had been tapping, and now held his heart, he knew there was no fighting it. Love. Such a lark!

Feeling rather giddy, Armand hadn't been able to resist step-

ping into Lady de Winter's salon as he'd come upon it in the
Palais de Justice.

A full-nasal citrus assault attacked from a table of peach-
colored sachets. To Armand's right peppermint oil boiled on
a silver salver set above a low flame. Gardenia clouded invisibly
overhead, whether it was the scented hats or the streams of
dried flowers he could not be sure. Everywhere scented gloves,
stockings, and perfumed corsets competed with his senses.

It was enough to make a man prefer a room full of snoring.

"I believe this may be what you are looking for, *mon chèr.*"

Lady de Winter displayed a pink glass pot etched with slender
narcissus upon her palm. Her scarlet lips pouted as she perused
Armand. In her violet eyes danced a teasing challenge.

He reached for the pot of face cream, but jerked away when
Lady de Winter ran a fingertip across his wrist.

"So jumpy you are, *mon chèr.* Come now, I'll not bite. Not
too hard, at least."

It wasn't her bite Armand was worried about. It was the
challenging glint in her eyes and the creamy cleavage that
blossomed from her dress. She wore her gown low enough to
expose the rosy aureoles on each breast. The style at court.
Appreciated by any man with eyes. And a cock.

"I'll take it," he said hastily.

"You'll take this?" She tapped a finger on the side of the
pot. "Or this?"

Armand felt the saliva pool in his mouth as he watched her
draw a fingertip over her décolletage. When she passed over
the mounds of rising and falling flesh, Lady de Winter sucked
in a gasp. The instant awareness of her pleasure bolted Armand
with a stiffening in his breeches.

"Chéri?"

Damn it anyway, he was acting the fool! He had exactly
what he needed waiting at home for him. Armand grabbed the
face cream and pulled his purse out from inside his doublet.

"I said I mustn't remain long. I've things to attend. Here you are, Lady de Winter. Three pistoles?"

She sighed, obviously disappointed at his disinterest. "I could make it two if you were not in such a hurry."

Armand counted the coins in his hand. Just enough for the face cream and perhaps two more meals. The discount she offered would certainly help now that he had Madeleine to concern himself with. He was by no means a wealthy man. Quite the pauper thanks to the redirection of half his wages.

"Your wife would most appreciate a few sous saved so that she may purchase more of my face cream when needed," she said with a hopeful rise to her voice.

"Perhaps."

The warm slide of Lady de Winter's hand across his cheek reminded Armand of the way things had been when he hadn't a care for a woman's virtue or her well-being. Things had changed though. He now knew what it was like to share himself with a woman he loved.

Love? Yes, love.

"No time for a discount today, Lady de Winter. But I thank you for your generous offer." He tipped up her chin and smoothed his thumb along her crimson lip. "I am truly a fool."

Satisfied with his confession, Lady de Winter removed only two pistoles from his opened palm and pressed a kiss to his cheek. "You may be a fool, *chéri,* but your wife is one lucky lady."

Madeleine slumped against the wall, devastated. She'd checked everywhere in Armand's cozy two-room apartment, finding nothing that could be linked to Fouquet. She distinctly recalled seeing Armand handle a parcel of papers in the carriage last night as they'd fled Vaux. That must be where Armand had gone this morning. The goods had already been delivered.

That spoiled her plans to blackmail Fouquet.

She'd had a most clever inspiration while dressing this morning. She had to be prepared, should Armand return with intentions of turning her in as a spy. For as much as she despised Fouquet, wouldn't it be fabulous if she could turn around and assist Armand in proving the financier's crimes? That would certainly redeem her betrayals in Armand's eyes. And it would make her feel all the better to know she was finally working for the right side.

But then something else occured to her. Armand had no clue regarding her previous marriage, or the fact that de Pellison had plans to strip her fortune away from her.

How could Armand trust her if she did not reveal all? And *could* she reveal all? They had only just become lovers. Their relationship was still so new. And with her betrayals looming like a dark cloud over his head, she could not overwhelm him with another revelation.

That she had been married didn't appear to bother him. Armand knew Pierre was dead. What could he possibly hold against a dead man? And he knew he was the only man she had ever lain with. But Armand had no clue about the terms of Madeleine's inheritance. Would he understand when he finally knew that she was the very thing that had once served his thievery? A rich widow.

How ironic. But Armand would not see it that way.

And so she had hoped to secure something to keep Fouquet's threats from boiling to fruition. But now she had nothing. Not even a slip of evidence.

Confused, and seeking a gentle soul to share her worries, Madeleine sought out solace.

Valérie might have appeared almost chipper were her face not sallow and the circles around her eyes a deep maroon. Stephan lay upon her lap, and a maid was helping to lace up her chemise as Madeleine entered the room. The babe had presumably just finished nursing, though the presence of Valérie's wet nurse must mean her milk was drying up.

"Madeleine!"

Forcing a cheery smile and a light step, Madeleine hugged her cousin and kissed her pale, salty forehead. Stephan cooed as she tickled his pea-sized toes while the maid handed him over to the wet nurse. Valérie dismissed the women and her son, and beckoned Madeleine to sit bedside on a chair.

"You are improving." Madeleine said it as a statement, in hopes of lifting her cousin's spirits. "I wager a few more weeks will find you and Stephan dancing outside in the gardens, having a fine time. The roses climbing your pergola out back are in bloom right now."

"My dear Madeleine, you needn't humor me. The surgeon was here last night, poking and prodding every portion of my anatomy. The consumption rages inside my feeble body, and my humors are dreadfully misbalanced. He said my lungs are filled with fluids. I may have less than a fortnight."

"Don't speak like that, Valérie. Surgeons are known to be wrong. Why, look at your color this morning, all rosy and cheery. Perhaps I should inquire about a different surgeon for you?"

"The color in my cheeks is courtesy of Lady de Winter, *mon amie,* and the cheer is only because I have missed you so. You mustn't fret, cousin, I've already placed my fate in God's hands." With that, she gestured to the bedside table, where Madeleine spied her ivory-beaded rosary; she handed it to Valérie. "I am ready to go to Him. I am."

Horrifying to hear such a statement from one so young. Madeleine swallowed, fighting a sure flood of tears.

"Valérie, you are a far stronger woman than I."

"It would be the easiest thing in the world, this business of dying . . ." The rosary beads clicked against one another as she pressed her hand to her breast. "If only I hadn't a child to leave behind."